THE LEGACY
OF THE
DIAMOND KING

Roy A. Clark

with Greg Smith

Black Lake Press
TELL YOUR STORY
BLACKLAKEPRESS.COM

Black Lake Press

TELL YOUR STORY
BLACKLAKEPRESS.COM

Cover design by Amanda Clark.

Published by Black Lake Press of Holland, Michigan. Black Lake Press is a division of Black Lake Studio, LLC. Direct inquiries to Black Lake Press at *www.blacklakepress.com*.

ISBN 978-0-9824446-4-1

IN GRATITUDE

To my parents who said I could do anything, if I just tried hard enough. Thank you. Every once-in-a-while I still believe you. I couldn't have done it with out you.

To my wife Amanda whose undying support keeps me going every day. You are the hero of the story.

To my In-Laws. Thank you for letting me marry your daughter and for all the help in supporting our dreams.

To my children who have endured all my jobs, emotions, lectures, and questions. This book is for you and your children.

To my friends...where do I start? Your words of encouragement, hope and truth are always on my mind. Just not for very long.

To my co-author Greg. You convinced me and continue to do so. Thank you for arguing, listening, believing, and writing my heart.

*To my mentors and mentees. Clearly you have shaped my life and I am wealthier for it.*Glossary

Saggezza (sad'dzettsa)_____: wisdom

Diamante (dia'mon-tay)_____: diamond

Aquila (akwila)_____: north winds

Jalous (zhal-use)_____: envious

Ragnar (Rãg-nar)_____: strong army

Ferox, Feroxan (fare-o) (fare-ox-en)   : fierce

Ferus (fare-us)_____: wild, thorny

Regno, Regnian_____: I reign
(régno) (régnian)

Castello di San Michele_____: castle of San Michele
(kastello dee san san michele)

Monte Saggezza_____: ascent of wisdom
(mon-tee sad'dzettsa)

Avigliana _____: town in the Susa Valley
(avig-lee-ah-na)

*"Teach us to number our days aright,
that we may gain a heart of wisdom."*

I am the wealthiest man in the world.

You might not recognize me or be able to tell by my appearance. But nonetheless, it is true.

How? This is my story...

CHAPTER 1

Work was harder than usual that day. I had just spent the morning having breakfast at the local Fat Boys Diner with Todd and Brandon, two employees turned close friends over the years. Friday was our usual morning to meet over some of the world's best French toast and hot coffee. The food was great, but the conversation was difficult. That morning I had to let them know I wouldn't be able to pay for their health insurance anymore.

"Refill?" One of the locals took his turn and made the rounds.

"No thanks." I kind of mumbled as the three of us sat there, with not much to say.

They were gracious and encouraged me to keep trying.

"This is no time to give up." Todd looked at me like only a friend with history can. Brandon nodded and smiled, he was thinking about his wife and two kids. Eventually he looked up. "Yeah, don't give up."

Taking your own advice some days can be the hardest thing to do. We finished up the last pieces of bacon and headed off to work. I paid the bill. It was the least I could do.

That afternoon, with nothing left to do but make cold calls and hear from bill collectors, I bailed out around 2:30

and went home. I care deeply for my employees. Leaving work early was as much to avoid my friends as it was to avoid all the responsibilities of owning a company. It's not my nature to run away, but that day it was just too much.

The drive home was a blur of questions as I wondered about how I was going to pull myself out of the pit I had dug myself in. As I pulled into my driveway, trying to avoid the scooters, bikes, and basketballs, I saw a stack of brown boxes piled up on my front porch. I knew my wife was out picking up the kids from school and I thought to myself, *If she's leaving me, she forgot half her stuff.* I laughed to myself. I joke when I'm stressed. I parked the truck in the driveway and walked up to the front porch. From the UPS stickers, it was clear that it was a delivery of some sort. Had the stress driven my wife Amanda out of her mind? Had she snapped and ordered everything on the IKEA website?

On top of the pile was a certified letter from an impressive sounding law firm from New York City, marked "Express." It was addressed to me. Everything was. A mountain of boxes, all sent to me Next Day Air. I had no idea what it was all about. The letter seemed like the easiest place to start. I tore open the envelope and found a hand written letter.

It read...

Dear Grandson,

If you are receiving this letter, then I have passed on and my grateful life has come to an end.

Take the knowledge I once possessed and enjoy the life I once had.

Here is your opportunity to become the wealthiest man in the world.

When you're ready, take the heirloom to Sacra di San Michele.

If your father is still alive, please let him know that I never stopped loving him.

-- Your Affectionate Grandfather.

P.S. Forever remember the legacy of the Diamond King

A letter from my mysterious grandfather that I barely knew. I hadn't seen my grandfather in at least thirty years. There was some ugly family history, what we like to call, "dysfunctional." In our case, it was a nice way of saying most of us in the family had chips on our shoulders and never talked to each other. My grandfather, though, hadn't been like that. I knew he had some sort of career as a consultant, or something, and had spent most of his time traveling the world. But he and my dad had stopped talking to each other when I was in grade school, and we hadn't seen grandpa since.

Still, I was curious. My dad's refusal to answer any questions about him only stoked my imagination over the years. I'd hang onto little tidbits of information. An offhand comment from one of my aunts that grandpa had been in Africa, or a Christmas card sent from Brazil. My adolescent mind had fantasized that grandpa was a secret agent or a mercenary or a pirate. Over the years, though, the mystery had faded. We were just another screwed up family, like hundreds of millions of other screwed up families. Nothing to see here, keep on moving.

I quickly moved the boxes in the garage. Twenty-seven in all and one green foot-locker with a padlock. "Hmm, grandpa must have been in the military," I told myself. Interesting. I really didn't know. The "dysfunction" between my dad and my grandfather meant that we never, ever talked about grandpa, as long as I could remember. I didn't know anything about him.

It took me half-an-hour to haul in all of the boxes. Every one of them was pretty heavy. I was sweating and expected Amanda and the kids to arrive any minute. I was looking forward to telling her about the mysterious shipment. It would be a welcome distraction from the conversations of work and worry. Maybe we could avoid talking about how the business was going down the toilet and our inevitable bankruptcy.

I knew starting a business would be tough and that running one could be even tougher. But to shut one down? We hadn't even pulled that trigger yet, and this was already the hardest thing I'd ever gone through. If something didn't change soon, we'd be shutting the doors within weeks. Bankruptcy wouldn't be far behind.

We had rolled up our sleeves and given it the old college try, looking for some way to maintain the employees' health insurance and still keep the company afloat, but in the end, we just couldn't find a way to make it work with benefits. My employees didn't blame me. They knew the economy sucked and that it was happening to businesses all around us, but I was still haunted by all the "shouldas, wouldas and couldas." Was I out of line taking that trip? Did we really have to buy a second car? That old fishing boat? Now they felt more like anchors around my neck. My employees didn't criticize my choices, at least not to my face. But what were they all thinking now? Doubt gnawed at my gut. I didn't plan enough; I thought about myself too much, there must have been something I could have done differently to avoid being in this place.

My wife and I had done all right, I guess. We never had too much, but most of the time we felt like we didn't have enough. We'd gambled everything on this new business, hoping we could work our way into a better life. The day our incorporation papers had arrived, we toasted with cheap champagne from the corner convenience store. It wasn't so much that we were trying to get rich; we just felt somehow we were destined for...more. Neither of us knew for what, exactly, just "more." We knew that we mattered to family and friends, and that was important to us. But we wanted to do something important, something significant: write a novel that changed the course of history, invent a cure for cancer, or run an orphanage like Mother Theresa. Amanda is more practical than I am. She tells me I'm a romantic dreamer. And yet I think that both of us had hoped that if the business took off we could invest a lot of the profit into worthwhile projects. We'd restore neighborhoods that had lost hope, give scholarships to brilliant young kids who could change the world, rescue children from bleak futures–things like that. We knew that we'd never run some wealthy foundation and be able to give money away, but we hoped that our business could do the same sort of thing in a smaller way.

We had sunk nearly fifty thousand dollars—everything we'd been able to save or scrape together throughout our lives—into the business. That didn't include the thousands upon thousands of dollars taken out on loans mortgaged to our home. We were so upside down the blood was running to our heads. We were a heartbeat away from losing everything. We needed a miracle, and we needed it fast.

CHAPTER 2

"So why can't I park the car in the garage this time?" Amanda said with a slight smile. I told her that my grandfather had left me a bunch of boxes and a letter and that we could chat after dinner. She looked at me skeptically.

"Maybe it would be better after the kids went to bed. I don't actually know what's in them." I said, hoping she would drop it for the night.

After we convinced the kids to go to bed early, I started in with all the boxes. Even though I had too much on my plate with work and family, I now had a great excuse to let my mind wander about something else. With all that was going on with the business struggling, my new adventure was hardly the priority. I didn't have time left over to dive into someone else's life, someone I never knew, even if he was my grandfather. An hour later after rummaging through a couple boxes of books and journals, I crashed into bed wondering about what I was doing.

"Well?" Amanda waited.

"It's just a bunch of books."

"He left you a library?"

"I don't know babe," and that was it. Conversation over.

Saturday morning, after I had taken the kids out for donuts, Amanda agreed to take them with her to run errands. She always had a way of knowing when I needed a little space to think and dream. I grabbed a cup of coffee and eagerly made my way back into the garage and started back in with all the boxes. As I continued to open box after box it became apparent that the majority of my inheritance was to be a bunch of boring books, journals, letters, and receipts. It was crazy. All my grandfather had left me was a bunch of written, dated information. Was that all he wanted me to have?

Then I remembered the letter: *"Take the knowledge I once possessed and enjoy the life I once had."*

Hmmm. What does that mean? I wondered. *Maybe he meant this to be the sum total of his wisdom. OK, nice gesture. I guess it's the thought that counts.* But at that point, I really could have used something a little more—how shall I say it? Practical, valuable, tangible. Cash, for instance, would be good. Other people's grandfathers leave them a wad of dough or a farm in Iowa. I got some consultant's books and notes. *Gee,* I thought, *my lucky day.*

Paging through, I noticed that quite a few of the documents referenced something called "The Saggezza Foundation." I had no clue what that was.

Frustrated and bored, I dug around absently in the files, and started to find thank-you notes. Lots and lots of thank you notes, from all sorts of people. Hand written and filled with hope. In another box I found receipts. Not the kind of receipts you get when you buy something but the kind of receipt you get when you donate something. Again, many of the notes and receipts mentioned "The Saggezza Foundation."

I began to look at the numbers, shuffling through the receipts. So many thousand here, so many tens of thousands there. I didn't need a calculator to see that he had donated millions of dollars. I was astonished. My grandfather was wealthy and I didn't even know it. In fact, the more I dug the more it appeared that he was enormously rich. And all he left me was a bunch of books and files. Life was playing another cruel joke on me.

I felt myself resenting him, just like I felt myself resenting my own father at times. I wasn't angry, and I didn't want to be ungrateful, but it just seemed like he could have passed on something a little more valuable to me. I had to stop. I was getting a little too frustrated. All this junk, and now I couldn't even fit one of the cars into the garage. Just what was I supposed to do with all of it?

As I made my way back into the house, I noticed hiding under a couple of those brown boxes was that old green military footlocker. *Was he in the military?* I wondered. *What's going to be in that one? His medals and discharge papers?* Could be cool, I guessed, but not much of an inheritance.

I went inside, got a drink and stood in front of the refrigerator, tried to decide if I was hungry or just thirsty. I'm told that most of the time you think you're hungry, you're really just thirsty. I grabbed a glass of water. I thought of the footlocker. "Oh, why not," I mumbled as I went back out to the garage.

The footlocker had a lock on it. Maybe there was a key buried somewhere in one of the twenty-seven boxes, but I didn't feel like looking for it. I got a pry bar from my tool bench and pried the hasp right off.

I was hit with a pungent smell and found basically what I had expected: pictures of comrades, more books–military manuals on airplanes, and engines—and a couple yearbooks with signed pages from what appeared to be his friends. Some really ratty looking guys—with friends like that I would hate to think who his enemies were.

Then, underneath some old shirts in the top left corner of the footlocker, there was a wooden box about four inches square by about three inches thick. It didn't rattle when I picked it up, although you could hear something inside, and it wasn't necessarily pretty. It looked very old and very plain. I examined each side and found what looked like an old European crest engraved on the bottom of it.

It appeared as if the lid slid up and off, so that's what I did. What I saw next took my breath away. My heart pounded and my hands began to shake. There, in a perfect circle, much like on a watch face, were twelve very large, exquisitely cut diamonds.

I began to cry. Somehow the tears had broken through the many months I had spent numbly wondering if we were going to make it. I had never seen anything like it. As the sun pierced through the garage window it hit the diamonds. The reflections of light danced with the most brilliant display of colors on the walls. I sat down to catch my breath and gain my balance so that I didn't drop them.

I didn't know a lot about diamonds, other than picking out Amanda's engagement ring, but I knew that these were huge and brilliant. I had a feeling that I was holding a fortune in my hands.

"We're saved," I whispered.

The stones were loose, and rested on what appeared to be a black wooden tray. Each diamond was set into a divot that held it perfectly in place. A scarlet ribbon stuck out the left side of the tray as if used to lift it up. Once again, my hands began to shake. I poured the diamonds into the lid that had some letters on the inside. I didn't take much time to see what they were as I continued. I set the lid, now filled with diamonds, down and gently pulled up the tray. Underneath was a little scroll, made out of a leathery sort of paper—vellum. A thin golden ring held the scroll together. The paper was old and worn. I slid the ring off and gently unrolled it. I could see the oil residue of countless fingers that had unrolled the scroll over the years.

The moment I began reading, my heart sank.

It said, "The Saggezzan Rules."

Rules? I didn't want any stupid rules. I wanted to save my business, keep our house, and take care of my employees. No rules. Especially unknown "Saggezzan" rules, whatever they were.

"Rule #1: YOU MAY NEVER SELL, TRADE, OR INVEST THE DIAMONDS."

Ahhhhh, I groaned inside. There went my quick fix, my miracle, the ability to resolve my problems in one fell swoop. It was amazing. Within a matter of moments after seeing the diamonds and with out even thinking things through, I had already spent the diamonds. I had invested some, sold some for cash, and who knows, maybe even given one away. I didn't really even think about it. My business was saved, my employees were back, and we all had health insurance.

There are rules that I'm supposed to follow, I reminded myself. But at that moment, I wasn't in a rule-following mood. "Screw the rules," I said out loud, then looked around to make sure no one heard me. I looked back down at the scroll. *Rules? Whatever.*

"RULE #2: YOU MUST PASS ON THE DIAMONDS TO A RELATIVE IN WHOM YOU TRUST."

Oh, this was rich: My grandpa, who didn't even know me, trusted me enough to pass something this valuable on to me? Wow. Our family was even more dysfunctional than I thought.

Why me? If he was going to pick someone in our family, why not my younger brother? He was much smarter and always seemed to make all the right moves in life. Maybe grandpa picked me because I was older? Did age have something to do with it? What about my cousins? I wasn't sure whether they knew Grandpa any better than I did.

And why lay this "trust" thing on my shoulders? I was sick of responsibility. *Let someone else be responsible for a change,* I thought.

"Rule #3: YOU MUST ACCOUNT FOR THE DIAMONDS EVERY EVENING."

I had no idea what that meant. Honestly, after the first two rules, I'm not sure I wanted to keep reading.

I set down the scroll and took a drink. *This is getting a little weird* I thought to myself. I picked up the box, the lid, and the open scroll and headed inside. I made my way down the stairs into our "home office," which meant my computer on a folding table next to the guest bed, where the floor was covered with the kids' toys. I needed some time to think before my wife got home and the kids started running around here with their friends asking all kinds of questions.

I got myself situated in front of the computer after scratching some Play-Doh off the desk and excusing Ken and Barbie from my office chair. They didn't look happy, so I threw them on the bed. "Good luck, Ken." I chuckled.

I bumped the mouse and the screen saver popped up. It was a picture of the family. It was one of those great pictures of us on vacation. The only vacation we had taken last year.

I looked at the scroll again. "Let's keep going". Underneath the rules was another section entitled "Instructions."

Finally, there was going to be some explanation.

1. Turn the lid upside down. Pour the diamonds into the lid.

"Well, I did that already," I said to nobody.

Embossed in the wood lid were lines of faded gold down the center and across the middle forming a cross. In each corner was a letter.

I assumed they had meaning, so I kept reading.

2. You must account for the diamonds every evening. Every evening you must ask yourself two questions.

First, Where did you invest your time?
Second, In whom did you invest your time?

With it all starting to be fleshed out, I realized that this was big, a little too big for me, and I began to wonder what my grandfather had done. How did he pick me? Why did he pick me?

3. Place the diamonds in the appropriate corner of the lid.

Each diamond represents one perfect, working hour, given within each day. Each diamond is filled with opportunity. Each diamond represents all of our responsibility. Each diamond represents sixty minutes that is given to every man, woman, and child regardless of tribe, color, or nation; regardless of wealth or poverty.

It was quiet and I was silent. I sat there thinking about my days and the hours that I had invested or wasted. Immediately, I wondered about Brandon and Todd and how they felt I invested my hours. I thought about my wife and kids and wondered, *What did they think about the hours that I invested?* I'm not sure I ever thought about the individual hours that I had invested, or even thought about it as investing. Sure, I was familiar with the phrase, "spending time." But it never went past that. You wake up, you go to work, you come home, you have dinner, you hang with the kids, talk with the wife, check your emails, and go to bed. There were goals I was trying to achieve and dreams I had had about the business, although though recently it felt it was all falling apart, so you kind of get in a rut. I guess maybe that's what happened to me. So...there I sat, looking at the scroll, hoping that it would all start to make sense.

I didn't hear my wife pull up, but the kids slamming the car doors made my heart skip a beat. I could hear them screaming outside, just having fun. I imagined them chasing each other with sticks and throwing pine cones all around the yard. Amanda made her way up stairs with a bag full of groceries. "Hey Babe," she yelled downstairs. I responded in a daze. "Hey..."

Had I lost myself, my perspective on things? Was I living without direction? I never thought of myself as aimless or without purpose.

Amanda made her way back out into the garage to get more groceries. "A little help here would be nice."

I jumped up and put the box back together. We had a little safe in the basement, to hold everyone's birth certificates, insurance policies, and stuff like that. I hid the box in there. I needed more time to think. As I ran upstairs to go into the garage I could see Amanda kneeling down to pick something up.

"What's this?" She looked at me with one brow up and her face squinted on the other side.

It was the gold ring that held the scroll together.

"Baby, we've a lot to talk about."

"Really, what else is new?" she said with a half smile.

Talking to my wife was rarely difficult, although it had been a little more of a challenge with the finances being so tight. Transparency mattered to me, and so did the truth, so that night I showed her the box, the diamonds and the scroll. She always had good questions. I didn't always like her asking them when she did, because they were the kind of questions that were so obvious that I felt dumb because I didn't think to ask them first.

Her first one was just like that. "What do the symbols in the lid mean?"

"Good question." I had no idea. There was nothing more on the scroll or in the box. We packed up everything and both went to bed wondering.

CHAPTER 3

The next day we went to church, and I'd forgotten that we had signed up to serve lunch at the local homeless shelter. Sunday night, I drove our oldest to youth group, and then waited around to take him home. By the time I fell into bed I hadn't had any time to really think about how I'd invested my hours. I did fall asleep dreaming of how I'd spend the money when I sold the diamonds, though.

On Monday morning, I went to the garage and quickly rummaged through the rest of the boxes, gathering up some of the documents. In the bottom of the last box, underneath some books as if it was to be hidden or the last thing that I should find, was a large manila envelope with my name written on the outside. Inside were a number of items with some "could-be" answers to a question that had plagued my mind: why me?

I was surprised to find a couple newspaper clippings, the first one from my high school newspaper from an article I wrote entitled "Think About It." It was an article about how little effort it takes to make a big difference for some of the shut ins at the local rest home. I would visit them every once in a while, and it seemed to make them really happy, so I wrote about it. The second newspaper clipping was an article entitled, "No Giving Up," about a baseball game that

I had pitched in that had gone into extra innings. It wasn't that big of a deal. Quite frankly, I thought they made too much out of it. I threw an extra three innings since I hate losing, so I didn't want to give up. That's what I told the reporter. I don't remember my grandfather being there. He must have seen the article and saved it.

I smiled to find three thank-you cards written from me to my grandpa, for some birthday gifts he gave me. It was clearly before the big blow up or my dad would have never let me write him.

I discovered an old college transcript with some professors' notes highlighted. My grades were average at best, but the highlighted note was from a professor whom I respected. He wrote, "Keep asking great questions." I never really thought of it much, but I was always curious and loved to learn from this professor in particular.

There was a silver dollar just like the one I had found at my Grandpa's when I was a kid. I saw it lying on the floor next to the sofa, and I told my grandpa that I had found it. I remember him smiling and telling me I could have it. It was probably one of my favorite memories of my grandpa. What was he trying to tell me?

Two more items actually left me a little more confused and concerned than anything. The first was some computer software taped to what looked like a report of my Internet history, and the second was a photocopy of a loan that I had paid off a long time ago.

I wondered how my grandfather retrieved all this information: the transcript, the Internet report, and the copy of the loan. What did it all mean? Once again my head was swimming, and I had to get to work.

In all, it was nothing that impressive. *Our family must really be hurting if that's all it takes to get the inheritance from Grandpa,* I thought to myself. I stuck the items and articles back into the envelope and stuffed it into my daypack and tossed it into my truck. I headed to the office, thinking about the mystery in my garage and the supposed fortune in my basement safe.

I arrived to work before the others only to tell myself, *Another day on the sinking ship.* I was tired of bailing it out. I closed the door to my office and turned off the ringer to my phone. I started reading through my grandfather's documents more carefully.

At first it seemed like there was no pattern to them. He had apparently been everywhere. There were signs that he had traveled or worked or been involved in projects on every continent except Antarctica. I couldn't find any consistency, though. From what I could tell, he seemed to be either employed by or owned a company called United Engineering Specialties, Inc. His plane tickets, visas, and travel receipts were all paid for by or listed that as his business. I searched for it online; I found the most generic website I had ever seen. It said that the company provided "Engineering Consulting Services," whatever that meant, and had offices located in New York, London, Paris, Torino, Rio de Janeiro, and Tokyo.

I didn't know where to start in getting any more information about my grandfather. Should I just call the New York office and ask if anyone knew him, and could they please tell me who he was and what he did for a living? I suppose he was an engineering consultant, or something similar.

More curious were all the references to the Saggezza Foundation. It was mentioned frequently, but there was no clue about what it was. It seemed to be wrapped up in all his philanthropy. There were references in letters and thank you notes, but always in an indirect or evasive way, as if it were an inside joke, or a secret that occasionally slipped out in conversation between people who were inside the loop.

I started surfing the web, looking for any information on the Saggezza Foundation. I found a lot, but none of it was helpful. It was mentioned on websites along with Area 51, the Illuminati, and the Knights Templar. Some of the same sites also had grainy pictures of Bigfoot and maps of the Bermuda Triangle. Not a good start. From what I could gather, the Saggezza Foundation was some sort of international secret society that originated a thousand—some said two thousand—years ago. It was supposed to be incredibly wealthy, controlling vast assets across the globe and dabbling in every industry in every country. No one seemed to agree on what their aims or purposes were, other than that they stayed in the shadows and used their riches to advance their hidden agenda. Whatever that meant. Another kooky conspiracy theory. As a last thought, I checked Snopes.com, the site that debunks urban myths. They listed all the nutty stuff and rated it as "false."

So if the Saggezza Foundation was an urban myth, what were all these notes, letters, and the apparent millions of dollars used for philanthropy? What about the box of diamonds in my basement safe?

I leaned back, frazzled. I wasn't getting anywhere and had a sick feeling that the only way that I would make any progress figuring out the mystery that got dumped on my porch was to light the powder keg. I was going to have to ask my dad about my grandfather.

After about an hour of sitting and stewing, I called my dad.

"Hey Dad," I said in my usual tone.

"Hey," was all he said. I waited and he continued,"What do you need?"

"Nothing, just calling to see how you're doing."

"Good," and it was silent again.

"Hey, what are you doing tonight?"

"Why?"

"I was just wondering; I was thinking of stopping by."

"Why?" It was a little softer this time.

It was an awkward conversation, like most conversations with him seemed to be. It wasn't that we fought or had gone through some horrible falling out. We certainly had never had that sort of thing come between us, like what had caused my dad and his father not to speak to each other for thirty years. But we had very different personalities and could never find anything to talk about. I didn't know how to bring up the subject of grandpa, much less him passing away. I found it hard to believe that their relationship could have been so broken that he wouldn't even be notified when his father died. I just told him that I needed to come over and get his advice about some business issues. I could just imagine him shrugging on the other end of the call. He didn't ask anyone to get involved in his problems and didn't like it when other people asked him to get involved in theirs. Still, he said I could come over that evening. I offered to bring dinner.

That afternoon, I hustled home to change and stuff my backpack with some of the more intriguing books and papers from the garage that I had already gone through. I debated bringing the box of diamonds, and at the last second buried it carefully in the bottom of my pack. I kissed

Amanda and the kids and told them that I had a dinner meeting and didn't know when I'd be back. I stopped a few blocks from my dad's house to pick up dinner from our favorite Thai place, and half-knocked on his door as I entered with my arms full of take-out.

I never understood my dad's path in life, at least until that night. Somehow, when he was just out of his teens he gone his own way. He had "bushwhacked" his way through life: if he was at Point A and wanted to get to Point B, he wouldn't take the trail. He'd hack his way through the underbrush, following some path only he could see. The people he should have been traveling with—his parents, wife, kids, business partners, whomever—would be shouting at him from the trail, begging him to join them. In the case of my mom and my brother and sister, we begged him to come back to the trail and help us. No way; he had to do everything his way, and his way was always the hard way. And he always had to have some visible sign of independence on his body. He had a goatee before they were hip, almost like a middle finger shaved into his face. As soon as goatees became popular, he shaved his off. The same thing with tattoos, an earring, and any other way he could mark his rebellion. With all his trademarks becoming fashionable, today he was clean-shaven with a buzz cut. Go figure. What none of us ever got was what exactly he was rebelling against. He really was a "rebel without a cause," as far as I could see. He was contrary for the sake of being contrary. Instead of a chip on his shoulder, he had a big rock. I just never got what it was all about.

I was the opposite. I wanted to get along with everyone. At a deep, visceral level I wanted to connect with people. I wanted to know my wife, my kids, my partners, and employees and have them know me. I'm the guy who gets to know his neighbors, who starts conversations with waitresses, who buys a cup of coffee for homeless panhandlers and listens to their story. I wanted to know what had gone on between my dad and his dad that had been so bad.

Because our personalities were so different, my dad and I never really got to know each other. We were polite and friendly, but I needed to connect and he, for some reason, desperately needed not to. We were like trying to push the same poles of two magnets together: the resistance increased the closer we got, and we rarely made contact.

I wondered if that's what had happened between him and his dad. Apparently Grandpa had traveled around the world, connecting deeply with hundreds, maybe even thousands of people. At seventeen years old, my dad had moved a thousand miles away from his father and had isolated himself from Grandpa and everyone else.

I hoped that tonight I might be able to figure some of this out. I intended to try.

I called Amanda, and let her know that I was at my dad's and told her I was going to be late, maybe very late. "We have some difficult details to talk to about." Once again, she understood.

CHAPTER 4

As I walked through my father's door, we both nodded and said, "Hey."

My dad's place was like a post-college bachelor pad with mismatched furniture and absolutely no feminine touch. It wasn't that he didn't have money—he'd owned several businesses over the years and was at least comfortable—like with everything else, he just didn't care what anyone thought.

That included my mom. When the last of us kids moved out she realized that she was living with someone who didn't really care if she was there or not. She was where I got my need to connect, and she was never going to get what she needed from dad. She left and found someone who wanted to walk down life's trail hand-in-hand with her. Dad? It didn't faze him. He just kept on doing his thing. I guess if you never get close to anyone you don't miss them when they're gone.

He pulled out a six-pack of Pabst Blue Ribbon and we spread the food on the coffee table. I made an attempt to make small talk about sports. "Hey, did you see the game?" I didn't even know what game I was talking about. He followed the Lions pretty close, so I figured it was a safe bet. "No... no one is playing now son." He looked at me like he felt sorry for me and shook his head. I played sports growing up and he never missed a game but trying to talk about them was another thing altogether. One of my old friends would try to coach me every once in a while on how to "speak sports." He's a walking commentary on anything with a team and a ball. I once jokingly asked him, "Who was the second baseman for the Cincinnati Reds in 1972?" "Joe Morgan," he replied without even thinking, and then went on about a championship or something.

We dug into the coconut curry chicken and peanut sauce. After a few minutes the conversation stalled and we ate in silence. It could have been the PBR.

Now I was stalling. "You want some more?"

I got up to get a glass of water. He followed me, "Na, I'm alright." He made his way to the sink.

It was time to take the plunge and ask the questions.

So, as casually I could, I asked.

"Dad, do you know anything about the Diamond King?"

He froze. His plate slid out of his hands and crashed into the stainless steel sink. Then he caught himself as he almost fell into the counter. Everything froze again. He slowly looked up and over, right into my eyes. He didn't look sorry for me anymore.

"What did you say?" There was firmness in his voice like I just called him an "ass" or something.

I just looked at him and swallowed hard.

"What did you say son?" it was a little softer.

"Do you know anything, about the Diamond King?"

"Where did you hear about that?"

I didn't know what to say. "Uh, dad...I..." I turned and fumbled for my beer and then looked back at him and nodded toward the living room. "We need to talk."

He stood up and grabbed his can and quietly followed. He sat in his chair with his arms folded as if to say, Now spit it out.

I took a deep breath and told him about the boxes in my garage and then handed him the letter. I waited for what felt like an hour, just sitting there. Nothing. Then he spoke. "So he passed."

I could see his eyes starting to fill with tears, but his face was filled with anger. Now he was slowly shaking his head. I was scared.

"I don't know how he passed," I confessed. "I don't know anything, really. Where he worked, where he lived, what he did. I was hoping you could fill me in."

"He shipped me twenty-seven boxes. They were all full of books, mostly. There were papers from his travels and cards from all around the world."

Dad cleared his throat and seemed like he was composing himself. "Books, papers from around the world? Sounds like your grandfather."

I explained. "In his letter he said that he was passing on all that he knew, and that I was to take that knowledge and enjoy the life he had, to become the wealthiest man in the world. I don't know what all that means. Was he wealthy?"

He cleared his throat again. "If he was, I never saw it. He made a decent income, I suppose. His company sent him all around the world on business. But rich? Not that I ever saw."

"Maybe he meant wealthy in knowledge?"

"Probably," said Dad. "That's all I ever heard from him. Stories about far away places, long ago. Big ideas, visionary philosophies. People who changed history. Stuff like that. All the time, ever since I was a kid. When I got a little older he always wanted me to come along and see the places and meet the people. I went a couple times, but it just wasn't my thing. My mother always encouraged me to go, but I thought it was boring."

My dad stopped, like he was remembering something. "Our house was always full of books. I suppose that by giving you his books he meant to pass on his knowledge. He was pretty smart."

Normally, I need to talk everything out, to share everything I know in an attempt to engage the person I'm talking to. I can't play poker to save my life. But that night, sitting there with my dad, I felt like I needed to play my cards close. I wanted to know the truth about my grandpa, the diamonds, the donations, the Saggezza Foundation, all of it. But I didn't want to steer this conversation. I wanted my dad to tell me what he knew without manipulation.

He'd grown quiet. I thought that maybe I could get him talking by bringing up the Diamond King again, something to break the awkwardness.

"You know, in his letter he mentioned something that struck me as funny. I don't know what it means."

I waited. "What's that?"

It worked. I got him talking.

"Well, what's up with the Diamond King? What's that all about?"

He half-laughed as he shook his head. "You have to be kidding me. If there was one thing that drove me away from my dad, that was it."

"So you know who this Diamond King guy is?"

He nodded slowly and looked at the coffee table between us. "Yeah. I know."

I waited.

"Do you really want me to tell you about this? It's a long story, and quite frankly it's a complete waste of time."

"Yeah, Dad. I really want to know. I'm trying to understand what Grandpa said in his letter and why he left me some of the things that he did. I want to hear all of it."

Dad got up and grabbed another beer. He came back and stood by his chair but he didn't sit down. "My dad told me this story over and over and over. Some kids grow up memorizing baseball players' batting averages. Little Jewish kids learn to recite the Talmud. Me? My dad made me learn the story of the Diamond King. He would bring it up all the time, finding ways to apply it. There would be some event, maybe in the neighborhood, or at school, or on the TV news, and he'd say, 'Does that remind you of something? Remember the time that the Diamond King...?' Stuff like that. It was never supposed to be written down. Once he told me that writing down or publishing it was, 'Against the rules.' I asked him what that meant, but he'd only say that someday I would be ready to know the rules. It seemed crazy to me. Other times he'd check me on it, make sure that I knew the story correctly. We'd be riding in the car together, or out working in the yard, and he'd ask me to recite parts of the story. He'd correct me if I got any part of it wrong and make me start over. He'd say that's the way ancient bards passed on stories and histories. It was all oral and they'd memorize it and train the next generation to memorize it.

"I grew to hate the story. My dad would be gone on some trip to somewhere in the world doing whatever he did —he was never very clear about it—and come home and want to test me on that stupid story.

"When I became a teenager and got mouthy enough to talk back, I told him that I thought it was a stupid story and that I didn't want to recite it anymore. He tried to be understanding, but he told me that the story of the Diamond King was the key to our legacy and our mission. I had no idea what he was talking about. Still don't.

"So...I'd had enough. I didn't ask for a legacy, and I sure didn't want a mission. I was sick of the story, and I was sick of my dad's talk about changing the world, serving others, and all the rest of it. By the time I turned seventeen it made me puke just to hear him bring it up, and I told him that. He'd plead with me, tell me that we had a purpose, and that I had a destiny. 'What destiny?' I'd shout back. He couldn't answer my question. He'd just say, 'You're not ready to know. But someday you can be, if you learn the legacy of the Diamond King!'

"The day I finished high school I went down to the recruiting office and enlisted. I never went back and I never looked back.

"Your grandfather was a bright man: well read, well traveled. He was also crazy as a loon. He bought into these crazy legends and conspiracy theories. Maybe you've heard of the Saggezza Foundation? It's supposed to be an ancient secret society, like the Illuminati or the ancient astronauts or something. Well, the Diamond King story is a legend about the origins of the Saggezzans, in a distant past in some faraway land. He made me memorize the story, but I never got it, and I always thought it was bunk.

"So, now he wants you to get wrapped up in this nonsense, to get your head spinning with fables of kings of old, huh?"

"Well," I said, glad that I hadn't told him about the diamonds, "I'm trying to make sense out of all the information he sent me. Goofy legend or not, maybe it'll help me sort it all out. And what did you mean you weren't supposed to write it down? Did you?"

"I did. In fact, your pack rat mother found it and put it in one of those boxes of junk she left me out in the garage. When I was a kid, I wrote it down and showed it to my dad before I knew it was one of the crazy rules. He told me to get rid of it, but I never did."

"Well, what's the story?" I said as if to egg him on.

"You're sure you want me to recite this? Again, I'm warning you that it's a very long story."

"Yeah, I want to hear it."

"OK, you asked for it. Go to the bathroom if you need to and settle in. This is going to take a while."

My dad closed his eyes and exhaled as he sat down in his chair. He composed himself and took a deep breath, like he was loading the story into his mind, and he began to tell me the most extraordinary tale...

CHAPTER 5

There was once a young prince who inherited a great kingdom called Monte Saggezza. It was a land of steep hills between river valleys that ran down to fertile, coastal plains. From the glaciers of the Ferus Mountains it took a week on horseback to wind through the kingdom to its naturally sheltered ports on the warm Southern Ocean. Monte Saggezza was a prosperous country of farmers, craftsmen, and merchants whose ships traded throughout the world.

The capitol of Monte Saggezza was Avigliana, hard up against the kneecaps of the Ferus Range. It was a town of red tile roofs and buildings of warm sandstone, full of plazas with fountains and many trees. The people of Avigliana brought art, craftsmanship, and passion to everything they did. Their markets sold goods from every nation and their church buildings soared upward in graceful arches, illuminated by brilliant stained glass windows. The Parliamentary Assembly stood in the center of Avigliana, and in its halls and courtyards, officials worked to keep the kingdom healthy and wealthy.

The kings of Monte Saggezza did not live in Avigliana. By law and tradition, for more than a thousand years they had kept residence high above the town in the Castello di San Michele. It sat perched on a hill so steep that, from its walls, one could look almost straight down upon the red roofs of the town almost two thousand feet below. From the castle one would also see the snow-covered peaks of the Ferus Range towering right overhead, with glaciers tumbling between rocky crags to where they melted into waterfalls that could be heard from the castle, only an hour's hike away.

The first kings of Monte Saggezza had built their castle high above Avigliana to provide protection and a place of prayer for the people. The fortress provided a secure base from which to defend the entire foothill region. In times of war the citizens could take refuge in the great network of tunnels beneath it, which were full of weapons and supplies, as well as underground workshops, bakeries, and winepresses. The deeply religious Saggezzan kings could also devote themselves to prayer and study, and the people of the land had come to expect their rulers to be moral, as well as military, leaders.

The kings of Monte Saggezza had all the ordinary duties of kings everywhere, plus two rather unusual ones. First, they were to visit each of the principal towns in the kingdom once every year. When they visited, they would stay for a couple of nights, getting to know the townspeople and their concerns. They would meet with local officials and eat and sleep in the homes of the citizens. The kings would hold assemblies in guildhalls, plazas, and churches, reporting on the state of the kingdom and receiving the people's criticism as well as their praise. The royal visits usually took place during the month following the harvest, when everyone reflected on the year that was and looked forward to what was ahead. This custom kept trust and faith between the people and the kings high in the Castello di San Michele.

The other unusual duty of a Saggezza king was to travel alone, across the Ferus Mountains every year and find the summer camp of the king of Ferox on the high, northern plains. The Saggezzans were descended from the Feroxans. A thousand years earlier some of these warlike nomads had crossed the Ferus Range and settled in the valleys and down along the coast. They had learned new skills and a new way of life. The first king of Saggezza was the son of a Feroxan prince and a coastal merchant's daughter. Both sides remembered their shared ancestry and understood they needed each other. The Feroxans guarded the mountain passes and the wild lands to the North, preventing enemies from descending upon peaceful Monte Saggezza. In return, the Saggezzans allowed Feroxan traders to travel down to their ports, bringing exotic raw materials from the North and taking back the marvelous works of Southern craftsmen. The annual meeting of the two kings preserved the relationship and renewed the ancient bonds between the peoples.

In order for the two kings to recognize each other as the rightful sovereigns when they met each summer on those high plains, each side had given the other a gift many generations before. These had become heirlooms of both royal houses and signs of their authority. The kings of Monte Saggezza were given and carried the Sword of Ferox, a heavy blade made for desperate battles on cold, windswept plains. In turn, the Feroxan royal family had received an ingenious counting box, used by Saggezza merchants and architects to calculate large numbers. The square, wooden box—about a hand's length to a side—bore the crest of the House of Saggezza on the bottom of the box. Inside were little dividers and colored marbles. The various marbles represented different numerical values, and by manipulating them properly among the dividers a skilled user could solve and track complex number problems. Whenever the current kings met, they presented these heirlooms, gifts from each nation to the other, and recognized their distant royal cousins.

The current ruler of Monte Saggezza was King Bonum. He had come to the throne as a teenager when his father was killed in the last war the Saggezzans had fought, against the Island of Regno, sixty years earlier. Since then, King Bonum's wise management and steady temperament had brought six decades of peace and prosperity. He took his responsibilities seriously, and though he was growing old he had more energy and focus than men half his age. He rose early and eagerly to worship in the chapel of Castello di San Michele. As he walked briskly along its ramparts in the cold mountain air his advisors gave him reports while the sunlight crept down the hillsides to Avigliana's red rooftops. Many days he rode the five miles downhill to the Parliamentary Assembly to conduct affairs of state. He relished his visits throughout the kingdom each fall, and he carried the Sword of Ferox easily on his broad shoulders every summer as he crossed the glaciers alone to reach the northern plains.

The people loved King Bonum for what he did for them, but equally as much for what he didn't do to them. Unlike kings in neighboring countries, he imposed just limits on his own government. He never took more in taxes than was necessary for the protection and well-being of the kingdom. He instructed his officials to respect the citizens and their property and to not meddle in affairs that were none of their business. In deciding cases that came before him he usually ruled against busybodies and in favor of those whose honesty, creativity, and hard work had earned them the right to be left alone. In short, King Bonum treated the kingdom like a garden. He pulled weeds, kept out pests, and allowed it to flourish naturally. The people were happy and free, and that made them rich as well. Most Saggezzans were content to live peacefully and productively and to let their neighbors do the same. They loved and respected their king for letting them do so.

I never knew my dad to be much of a storyteller. As he told the story, it was like he was a different person. I wondered if it was my grandfather coming through him. He spoke with such ease and ability. I listened like a child at bedtime. For the first time ever, it felt like I was connecting with my dad.

CHAPTER 6

Not everyone in Monte Saggezza was content. Young people who had grown up during the reign of the elderly King Bonum were bored and, having never known any other way of life, took being rich and safe for granted. Generations of peace had created few true heroes, as many had become famous through art, sports or commerce. Young people came to mistake fame for heroism and worshipped these celebrities. They saw little reason to follow Saggezza traditions of saving and creating much from little. They longed for recognition, whether it was for real accomplishment or not, and they ignored the traditions that had blessed them more than they realized.

The most bored and spoiled young man in all of Monte Saggezza was King Bonum's son, Prince Diamante. The prince was young and his father was old, because the king's first wife and child had died in a shipwreck many years earlier. They had been going to visit her sister, who had married the king of the Island of Regno, Saggezza's main rival. King Bonum's grief had been deep and long, and he only remarried late in life. Prince Diamante was his only surviving heir and became the apple of the elderly king's eye. The heights of Castello di San Michele were a lonely place for a child, but it was Diamante's world and he conquered it zealously. The castle was full of endless nooks and crannies where a boy could hide to eat a treat smuggled from the bakery or eavesdrop on conversations. The system of tunnels and caves below the castle became his playground, and he knew every storehouse, workshop, and armory, plus all sorts of secret shafts and tunnels connecting them. He loved being the prince and what it let him get away with. He liked playing pranks on people who worked for his father and seeing their reaction when they realized that it was him and they could do nothing about it. Because the castle was built on such a steep height, its various rooms and areas were stacked almost vertically. Diamante was quick and agile and scampered up and down winding back stairways, ladders, and air shafts. Some days it seemed as if trouble was breaking out throughout the whole citadel at once, from the lowest storerooms to the highest ramparts.

Diamante was enchanted by the drama of the royal household. There was always something theatrical going on: the changing of the guard, receptions of foreign leaders, events in the chapel. When he was still a little boy he demanded a palace guard uniform so he could join in their ceremonies. The guards themselves were more irritated than flattered, since the boy liked to be the center of attention and to remind them that he was the prince. He pestered the officials for a role in banquets or concerts, always wanting to be visible and important. King Bonum was blind to most of this. His affection and hopes for the boy overwhelmed his judgment. He could not bear to deprive his son of anything or discipline him in any matter. Although his mother the queen worried that her son was undisciplined and disrespectful, she found it difficult to control such a headstrong prince in a castle full of officials and soldiers.

So Prince Diamante grew into an arrogant and unruly teenager. Even so, he was a remarkably gifted young man, and as his schooling began in earnest his skills became obvious to everyone. Tall and naturally athletic, he excelled at any physical contest. Sport was an important part of Saggezzan life, and Diamante became known throughout the kingdom as a standout competitor. He was a skilled boxer, runner, swimmer, and horseman. He won every archery contest that he entered, and his trainers helped hone his swordsmanship until it was as sharp as his blade. He was clever and had a gift with languages, which he practiced in the markets of Avigliana, with merchants from around the globe. Foreign dignitaries were shocked to hear this handsome youth speaking to them in their own tongue like a native.

Despite his talent, Diamante lacked judgment and self-control. He loved to gamble and was famous for his daring wagers with anyone about anything. He played cards with other wealthy youths at school, dice with soldiers, and placed sports bets with moneylenders in Avigliana. He wasn't as successful in games of chance as he was in athletic contests, and many welcomed him to their table, looking forward to taking some gold from the rich but reckless prince. He loved to cut a dashing figure and spent furiously on the most fashionable clothes and hairstyles. As much as the people loved and respected King Bonum, they began to gossip about and mock Diamante behind his back. Even so, his entourage swelled with youths that either shared his values or enjoyed the money and privileges that came with his friendship.

The old king loved his son dearly—some said unwisely —and made excuses for the prince's gambling, girls, and ungracious behavior. He would scold his son and pay his debts; the boy would hang his head and mumble some apology, and the matter was dropped. After a while, people stopped bringing bad news about the prince to the king, who interpreted the lack of complaints as a sign of the prince's improving maturity. His mother, who loved both the king and the prince, was caught between their strong personalities. She tried to counsel her son, but there were too many other influences on such a handsome and headstrong prince, and to him, her advice sounded only like nagging.

The prime minister of Monte Saggezza was a certain Count Jalous. He was a proud man, and although he had risen to the second highest office in the country he was full of envy and ambition. Jalous was certain that he could organize the kingdom even more efficiently, producing a more modern and glorious country that would be the envy of the nations around it. Bitterness consumed him as he imagined the arrogant and unserious young prince inheriting the kingdom.

Jalous feared King Bonum because of his popularity with the people, but he deeply resented Diamante. The prince's reputation rankled someone who took his own stature so seriously. As gossip about Diamante's foolishness spread, Jalous began to look for opportunities to spread and inflame the rumors. He knew that King Bonum would not be king forever, and although it was hard to foresee how things would turn out, it suited Jalous that the people not respect the future king as they did his father. He began to calculate ways to increase the power of the Parliament, and to diminish the prestige of the Crown after it came to rest on Diamante's brow. In the darkest hours of the night he fantasized about moving from Avigliana, up the hill to the Castello di San Michele himself, but he dared not allow himself to think such thoughts in the daylight.

And so the years crept on. The king got older and more tired; the prince got older but not wiser, and the count got older and more bitter. Monte Saggezza was quiet, rich, and quite unprepared for the tidal wave that would break upon it.

I began to wonder who I was, or who my dad thought he was in the story. Was my desire to do something great being born out of boredom or did I really want to help others?

My dad got up to stretch his legs. I was comfortable just taking it all in.

CHAPTER 7

As King Bonum's health failed, he tried to tidy up affairs so that his son would assume the throne of a kingdom in good order. As a ruler, he prepared the government for Diamante. But as a father, he worried that the prince was not ready to govern. He told himself that when the time came the new king would grow into his role.

One morning King Bonum was working in his private office, which was perched on a terrace over the outer wall, up a short circular staircase from the royal hall. He used this hour after breakfast to go over matters with a few advisors and to prepare for the day's events.

"I would like to meet with the prince today," said King Bonum, "please arrange a time for that. Perhaps after chapel this morning."

"Yes, sire," replied his secretary, who sent an aide to pass the invitation on to Diamante.

Two hours later, King Bonum walked out of the chapel into the small courtyard that looked down on the main gate and beyond that to the steep road up from the valley. The courtyard was crowded with worshippers, and King Bonum was engaged in conversation, but his eye kept scanning for Diamante. He had not seen him in the daily worship and wondered if he had left by the other door, which led downstairs to the main dining hall.

"Is the prince ready for our meeting?" he asked his secretary as the courtyard emptied.

"We were not able to locate him this morning, sire."

"Do you have any idea where he might be?"

"We believe that he is in town. I sent a message down the road, asking him to come up the hill as quickly as possible."

"This is most inconvenient. We will be tied up most of the afternoon with the ambassador from Montegavre."

The secretary looked nervous. "I did hear a report from someone who came up this morning. It appears that the prince was...occupied. I expect that our courier will conclude matters down there and your son should arrive around suppertime. I have arranged for Admiral Constante to take the ambassador on a tour of the gardens after supper and for you and the prince to have some time then."

"What has our prince been 'occupied' with this time?" asked King Bonum wearily as they descended the broad staircase that led to the level of the main hall. His secretary was silent. "Go ahead, Nico. Tell me."

The secretary once again looked nervous, but then shrugged. They had had this conversation too many times. "There was a party last night in Avigliana..."

"What do we have to deal with this time? A debt, a fight, or a girl?"

"I'm still looking into it, sire. Apparently, it's complicated."

"Isn't it always?"

That afternoon, King Bonum listened to the ambassador detail his concerns about trade and treaties. It was the necessary tedium of government, part of the hard work that the people of Monte Saggezza depended upon their king and officials to do. King Bonum found himself wondering how Diamante would handle these tasks. His son loved his privileges and the royal pageantry, but he had no sense of the responsibility that came with the crown. Would he insult some ally by leaving its ambassador waiting while he played the fool with hangers-on in the valley?

An aide whispered in the king's ear as they finished a light supper in a small gallery off the royal hall. He nodded to Admiral Constante, who graciously led the Montegavran ambassador out for a tour of the gardens.

He climbed a circular staircase and crossed a small terrace between the chapel and the outer wall. King Bonum could feel his age, and the gnawing pain in his stomach reminded him that he was trying to solve the final problems of his reign. He no longer walked between levels of the Citadel with the briskness of youth, and this evening it was not age that slowed his pace. He was prepared for his death, but was Diamante? He slowly climbed five more levels, moving between the towers and terraces, trying to find the words his son needed.

Diamante was waiting on the highest terrace, near the top of the tower containing the royal family residence. A small patch of grass surrounded a fountain, and potted plants made it feel like a floating oasis high amidst the granite walls of the towers.

King Bonum wished his son looked at least a little bit sorry after the trouble he had caused in the town yesterday, and all the work and money King Bonum's aides had spent cleaning it up. But the prince just looked bored.

A hundred feet below them, guards patrolled the walls. A thousand feet below there, birds rode updrafts off the valley floor, and another five hundred feet below that, the red tile roofs of Avigliana were broken by the pattern of streets and marketplaces. Overhead the peaks of the Ferus Range towered, the setting sun glistening on the glaciers. The future of Monte Saggezza was at stake, and this was the perfect place for them to face that.

The father told his son, "Do you know why I named you 'Diamante?' Because you came so late in my life, you were so precious to me. You still are." He watched a line of carts moving along the valley floor below, on their way to the coast. "Perhaps I value you so much that I have been an indulgent father. Now it is time for you to become the man you were born to be."

That evening King Bonum told Diamante that he was proud of his son's talent, but that this was not enough to make him a good king. A king, he said, must work and lead in the world as it is, not as he would wish it to be. He warned Diamante that a leader is bombarded by voices and information which rarely agree. King Bonum talked about how a good king must do what is right, not always what is easy or convenient. He advised Diamante to discover the truth in every matter and to craft solutions from facts, not fantasy. Fantasies and falsehoods were luxuries that kings could not afford.

"Leaders lead; if they can't lead they attempt to manage everything. Once they realize they can no longer manage, they make excuses. But once they run out of excuses they blame, and once they blame, they rarely lead again."

King Bonum tried to impress on his son that the king didn't own Monte Saggezza; rather that Monte Saggezza was entrusted to the king's care. The king was accountable to God and to the people to care for and cultivate his realm. He must spend his reign making the kingdom more secure, valuable, and just. That was his sacred duty, a holy relationship founded in time, trust, and communication.

"As king you must rise earlier, work harder and hold yourself to higher standards than anyone in the kingdom. It is your duty to be first in the attack and last in the retreat. You must never ask anyone to do anything or forgo anything that you are not willing to accept for yourself. You must listen more than you speak and speak only when certain. Once you do, people must know that your words are your bond. In times of plenty you must be sober and prepare for times of want. In times of want you must lead the people with vision and innovation and be thankful for the smallest portion at the table. You are not to rule the people for your own benefit; rather, you are to serve them for the benefit of the kingdom."

Diamante had always been bright and charming, and when he wanted to he could make a person feel like he was fascinated by what they were saying. That evening he appeared to be engaged in his father's advice, but King Bonum wondered if he was only being polite. Had he trained himself to look like he was paying attention?

"Diamante, you cannot be the king the land needs until you gain a heart of wisdom," said King Bonum. "It can't be bought or taught. It only comes with experience, and only then if you are determined to seek it. It is not enough to accept the crown. Your greatest desire must be to become a wise king and for wisdom to guide all your decisions."

"Of course," replied Diamante. "I dream of being wise like you." King Bonum hesitated, unsure if the prince was sincere. He thought of questioning him, but decided to continue.

"As I said, you are like a diamond to me. Consider a raw gemstone. It must be cut and polished for the brilliance locked inside to be set free. Everyone must be shaped by the pain of their experiences to achieve their full potential. It is even more crucial for those with great responsibility, because so much depends on the maturity of their judgment. When I became king I thought that I was ready, but I had no idea how demanding it would be. I learned some hard lessons during the early years of my reign, mostly by my own mistakes. My prayer for you—and Monte Saggezza—is that the cutting and polishing will not be too painful or expensive."

Diamante continued to nod and murmur agreement. King Bonum wondered if his son's lack of seriousness was only because he had not been faced with real responsibility yet. Perhaps, he wondered, he should have given his son some real duties to season him. For all his supposed wisdom as king, had he been a foolish father? Had his love for his son clouded his judgment and endangered Monte Saggezza?

King Bonum pressed on, determined to teach Prince Diamante what he needed to know in order to take the throne. King Bonum could feel in his body that that moment wasn't far off. He knew that he must use the time remaining to prepare the prince as best he could.

That evening on the terrace, as they seemingly hung in space over the kingdom with the sun setting behind the mountains, King Bonum taught Diamante the principles which the king had found led to a productive and joyful life.

He charged his son, as his father and as his king, to cultivate these qualities in himself. He promised him that if he did so, he would himself be a wise ruler and bring peace and prosperity to Monte Saggezza. Diamante nodded and dutifully wrote them down.

Their conversation lasted far into the night, with the king calling for fires to be lit in braziers to fight the chill. He persuaded, warned, pleaded, and did all that he could to impress upon the prince how important it was to Monte Saggezza that he live and rule by these principles. He made his son recite the Seven Saggezzan tenets from memory.

In the wee hours King Bonum's pain grew too much, and he concluded their time by embracing and kissing his son. Diamante left quietly, and neither of his parents could read his thoughts in the days afterward.

When the end was near, he called in the queen and Count Jalous and the rest of the court and commanded Prince Diamante to kneel beside the bed. Sitting up, the King gave his son a rich and royal blessing. A week later, King Bonum died from the illness that was consuming his insides.

That night the bells throughout the kingdom played a requiem for the king who had led his people in peace and prosperity for more than sixty years. As the news spread, people who had never lived under any other ruler expected that life would continue as it always had. Some hoped that things would get even better under the leadership of the handsome young prince. Others, like Count Jalous, wondered what might be possible for themselves. The next day at noon the bells sounded again, this time a joyful tune celebrating the crowning of the new king of Monte Saggezza.

I always wanted my dad to talk to me like that. I wanted him to teach me some kind of code we believed in or some values that we were committed to. We went to church growing up, but it was never really talked about. It's not like we had conversations about how to put what we believed into practice.

Maybe this would spark something in him that would create a desire to pass onto me what his father tried to pass onto him.

He continued...

CHAPTER 8

Diamante mourned his father appropriately, but he loved the idea of being king. At least he loved the attention and theater of it all. He wasn't really interested in the work of governing. The morning after his coronation ceremony, the aides and advisors began bringing him papers and problems; he found most of it complicated and boring. He quickly discovered that if he asked for and agreed with their advice, and then instructed them to carry it out, the work could be finished by lunch, and he could be free for the rest of the day.

Diamante did throw himself into some things. He had always found Castello di San Michele a dull, stodgy place. He also thought that many of the public buildings in Avigliana and around the kingdom were too old-fashioned. He began inviting famous architects and decorators from neighboring countries to visit and to give him proposals for change. He loved spending afternoons walking around various sites with them, making and taking suggestions for new building projects. He also cared a lot about his appearance and hired the greatest clothing designers from Saggezza and abroad to create his wardrobe.

Diamante loved to host parties for the most popular new artists, entertainers, and athletes. He threw himself into planning every detail, as the events became ever more elaborate. He particularly loved parties with themes; some were costumed, some were treasure hunts, some were multi-day entertainments that progressed through several towns, allowing the local people to see the celebrity entourage. He invited many of his famous friends to move into the palace with him and gave some of them positions in his administration. People began to wonder why these young entertainers were being given responsibilities for which they had no training or experience, but few dared to challenge the king's new appointments.

Castello di San Michele had beautiful gardens, which had taken generations to create. Arranged for miles among the hills around the palace, they were more like a series of massive parks. There were acres of flower beds arranged in shapes which could only be discerned from the palace towers. There were mazes made from fragrant hedges in which a person could get pleasantly lost for hours. A system of ponds and canals could be paddled in little boats while one conversed or contemplated amidst white swans and fish in every color of the rainbow. There were forests with private clearings for romance or an amusing game of lawn bowling. Orchards covered the hillsides with endless rows of fruit trees winding up into the base of the mountains. The Saggezzan Gardens were world famous, and foreign dignitaries always hoped for an invitation to view them.

Diamante had grown up around the gardens. As a child he had loved exploring them for hours. As an adolescent he loved hiding and making mischief in them. By the time he was a teenager the gardens bored him. Now that he was king he wanted to bring excitement and modernity to what he considered quaint relics of the past. Nothing delighted him as much as public attention. He got no thrill from sitting on a bench by a fountain in a secluded clearing or from wandering down endless rows of apple trees in the mountain orchard perched high over the town.

Now that he could, Diamante decided to alter the very nature of the palace gardens. He envisioned them becoming a crowded, energetic place, buzzing with fairs and events and crowds of admirers.

For centuries, these royal parks had been in the care of a master gardener, who traditionally reported directly to the king. Since before Diamante had been born the position was held by a small, wiry man named Don Verde. Perhaps it was the weathered face and hands, but Master Verde had always seemed old to the young prince. Don Verde had been a dear friend and trusted advisor to both King Bonum and Admiral Constante. The gardener was a quiet man who preferred to be outdoors overseeing his work crews, and Diamante never knew what to talk about with him.

In his first few months as king, Diamante began working with the new foreign architects he brought in to design the changes that he had imagined for the new gardens. Knowing Don Verde's commitment to the old ways and to the old gardens, retirement for Don Verde was the only hope for change. But if Diamante forced him into retirement the timing would be critical, for the kingdom loved the gardener nearly as much as the King.

Over the next two years Diamante's foreign architects transformed the hillsides around the castle. Arenas for athletic competitions and amphitheaters for concerts replaced gardens and orchards. Open spaces were cleared for public fairs with grandstands and booths to sell food and merchandise. One of the labyrinths was torn out for a lodge that catered to young celebrities. Another was restricted to visitors willing to pay an admission fee in the evenings, hoping to catch a glimpse of King Diamante or members of his entourage on one of their torch lit, costumed romps through the grounds.

The new fairgrounds were busy almost every night of the week. There were tournaments and parties and gaming and shopping. There was also quite a bit of heavy drinking. Thieves and prostitutes worked the crowds. Every morning workers swept the grounds of what had been the world-renowned Gardens of Saggezza, cleaning up the sleeping drunks, piles of trash, and puddles of vomit left behind in preparation for another night's festivities.

Similar projects went up across the country. Diamante granted licenses for gaming halls, saloons, and racetracks as they sprang up almost overnight in every town. Traditional Saggezzans were offended and angry, but the new establishments were tempting enough to be full every night. The king's endorsement made them seem more respectable, even as people worried about their loved ones and neighbors who devoted ever more time and money to these entertainments.

Diamante spent lavishly. He hired advisors, decorators, builders, managers, and inspectors of all sorts. He built public buildings, bought clothes and furnishings, and gave gifts and jobs to his ever-growing entourage. He threw parties, festivals, and tournaments, and moved about the major cities hosting all of them. He gave contracts to event planners and hired town criers and writers to promote his agenda and his reputation. It was an exciting time, and young people especially followed and admired his exploits.

Diamante was also burning through the fortune King Bonum had left him at a ferocious rate. By his second year as king, his advisors were warning him that the treasury was running low. To raise cash Diamante simply sold more licenses to gaming companies and borrowed from bankers on the Island of Regno. But for as much as he raised, he always spent more. As money became tighter, he increased taxes throughout the kingdom. He also cut spending on the navy and the network of fortresses that guarded the mountain passes, shifting the funds into more interesting new projects. Arguing with his advisors that the famous merchants of Saggezza were hoarding their wealth, he greatly increased the number of tax collectors in the marketplaces and ports.

My dad sat there and rubbed his eyes. I really couldn't tell if he had truly memorized the story or if he was making it up. He took a deep breath and started in again like he was ready to go over a big hill, as if he was mounting enough courage to get through something he wasn't sure he wanted to.

He looked at me as if to ask if he should continue. I nodded.

CHAPTER 9

Some tried to warn King Diamante that he was destroying the peace and prosperity that had made Monte Saggezza so world renowned. Admiral Constante had served King Bonum since they were both young men, keeping Saggezza's forces sharp and ready. The old admiral's respect for tradition and the monarchy made it difficult for him to raise the issue with his friend's son, but he knew that his sworn duty was to advise the king and protect the nation. If that meant that he had to point out mistakes in the king's policy, then so be it. That's the way King Bonum had always wanted it.

For weeks Admiral Constante asked Diamante for a private meeting, but the king kept making excuses to avoid a confrontation. He felt uncomfortable around the admiral. Aside from their age difference and opposite personalities, the admiral reminded Diamante of his father. Diamante felt like Constante was always on the verge of telling him that his father would have disapproved of his choices.

Although Constante would never have said such a thing, he thought it. As the Saggezzan economy began to crumble under Diamante's administration, Constante grew ever more concerned. What drove him to outright alarm was Diamante's decision to shrink the fleet and reduce the garrisons on the border forts. The admiral had spent his life keeping Monte Saggezza safe, and he knew that it had enemies who were jealous of its success. Those enemies had been probing Saggezza's defenses and harassing her merchant vessels for decades, and the admiral felt he had to make the king understand that his decisions were inviting trouble.

As was their custom, Master Verde and Admiral Constante met for early morning tea at the beginning of the week. It was a ritual that Diamante observed with a cautious and skeptical eye. Early in his reign he was invited to take his father's place at tea, but always had scheduled other appointments for that time.

"Constante," said the gardener on one such morning, "something needs to be done. Someone needs to tell him the truth."

"I know Verde, but it all seemed to fall on deaf ears."

"He has all his fathers drive and abilities, yet without purpose or wisdom."

Verde's heart sank as he thought about the young man whom he longed to see rule in the same fashion as King Bonum once had.

For years, Diamante had watched these two passionately discuss the needs of the kingdom with his father, always closing in prayer. But since becoming king, he regarded their passion for this kingdom as rejection of his authority.

Finally, to force a meeting, Constante used his influence with the palace guard, many of whom had served under him in the fleets and respected him immensely. One afternoon Diamante was riding around the fairgrounds that had been gardens, inspecting new excavations and construction. He was accompanied by a small group of architects, managers, advisors, and a couple of guards. The party approached a gate in a wall leading into what once had been a peach orchard but was now a muddy field full of taverns around a boxing arena. As they neared the gate, the captain of the guard and four of his men rode up briskly and announced that there was an urgent message for the king. The original guards escorted the king's entourage through the gate while the captain of the guard and his men offered to escort the king back to Castello di San Michele. As they rode through a small clearing in the trees, the guards pulled up their horses and turned around, guarding the entrances to the clearing. The king looked puzzled as Admiral Constante rode into the clearing at a walk.

"Admiral, what a pleasant surprise," said Diamante grimly. "But please, I must continue on. There is an urgent message for me."

"Your highness, I have the urgent message."

"Well?" said Diamante impatiently.

"My Lord, the kingdom is in grave danger."

"What has happened?" asked Diamante with genuine alarm. He had yet to face a crisis as king, and didn't want to.

"It is not what has happened, but what is happening," said Constante quietly. Decades of leadership had taught him that calm confidence can sometimes accomplish more than a harsh and alarming tone.

Diamante realized that the admiral had engineered this meeting for his own purposes, and he was annoyed. "Well, Admiral, since you have manipulated me and my guards to make some point, why don't you get to it."

"As you wish, my Lord. Here it is: the blessings of Monte Saggezza should not be taken for granted. They are not our birthright as Saggezzans. Our peace and prosperity has been hard-earned. They must be constantly maintained. For fifty years I have seen pirates looking for any opportunity to seize a Saggezzan ship. The only reason our trade fleet travels the world safely is that hard men defend them on the seas, out of sight of the good people of this kingdom. We enjoy the benefits of our navy, but few of our people realize what it costs for us to be the merchants of the world. This country, with its green and peaceful valleys, would be overrun if it were not for our alliance with the Feroxans and our own defense of the passes. There are barbarian tribes that would tear our wealthy towns and farms apart if those passes were clear and undefended for just one summer.

"There are other enemies, not just pirates and barbarians. The Island of Regno is crowded and has always lusted after our land. They are a powerful and sophisticated rival; do not think for a moment that they would hesitate to swallow us alive if they had the opportunity. I suspect that there are some in this kingdom, some even in your government, whose loyalty could be bought by the Regnians if they decided to make a move toward us."

Diamante was defensive. "Admiral, if you wish to defend your military expenses then I suggest you bring your concerns before the cabinet and parliament where these decisions are properly discussed."

Constante was undeterred, and continued in the same calm tone. "Sire, this is not an argument about money. I am appealing to you, asking you to understand the realities of this kingdom. Sire, you are responsible for keeping this kingdom safe. I advise you to take that role seriously."

"How dare you speak to me like that! I know my responsibilities."

"No sire, I don't think that you do. I don't think that you grasp what has been entrusted to you and what you are to do with it. I do not speak only of military matters. We all must understand and be faithful to our duties. Yours are heavier than anyone's, and they do not go away just because they are ignored."

"This is insolence, Constante! Perhaps it is you who does not understand your duty."

"On the contrary, sire. I have just tried to fulfill my duty to my king, my countrymen, and my oldest friend." With this, he turned his horse and walked slowly from the clearing, leaving Diamante angry and unsettled.

No argument could dissuade Diamante of the rightness of his vision. He continued to make deep and rapid changes in all aspects of the kingdom's life and government. Both the Admiral and Count Jalous watched and waited.

Diamante's character flaws were becoming the nation's weaknesses. Monte Saggezza had always been a place that cherished intrinsic value as found in the diligence of the farmer or the creativity of the craftsman. Its citizens enjoyed the fruit of their labors precisely because it was the fruit of *their* labors.

But the younger generation now devoted its attention to the escapades and affairs of Diamante and his celebrity entourage. Citizens of Monte Saggezza had always aspired to be successful in their work: a successful farmer or merchant or artisan. Now their children merely aspired to fame for its own sake. Young people tried to dress and act like Diamante and his friends, and dreamed of being invited to the parties and concerts held every night at the fairgrounds where the old gardens had been. The number of citizens who produced the wealth, which was taxed to pay for this lifestyle, shrank, and life became more difficult for everyone except for the few at the top of the social pyramid.

Monte Saggezza was still a beautiful country, nestled in fertile valleys between white mountains and a blue sea. Her towns and villages were orderly and charming. Her people still enjoyed a lifestyle that was the envy of her neighbors. But under King Diamante's reign, her heart was changing.

After his confrontation with Constante, Diamante began to regard the admiral's early morning teas with Verde as conspiratorial.

The time had come. Diamante decided it was time for Master Verde to retire. Maybe this would split the two elders' alliance, Diamante reasoned. He threw a banquet for the Master Gardener, and in front of the guests, he thanked him for his long and faithful service, presented some gifts, and awarded him a pension. It was very polite, but there was little warmth in the affair. The admiral was grieved to see this stalwart member of his generation, which had brought decades of peace and prosperity to the nation, dismissed with such insincerity by their new monarch.

CHAPTER 10

As king, Diamante was required by law to travel through the major towns of Monte Saggezza every year. He was to report to the people about the state of the country. The people would meet their monarch, and he would listen to their stories, hear their requests, and address their complaints. This tour traditionally took place in the fall after the harvest was brought in.

Whenever King Bonum came to a town during his fall tour, he spent a couple of days visiting businesses, hospitals, and homes. He learned about what was working in the kingdom and what wasn't. During the evenings, he ate in public halls and listened to the townspeople's criticism when necessary. He spoke with the church leaders, the trade guilds, and the local merchants. He toured farms and met with the local councils. In this way King Bonum had spent a few days in each town every year, taking more than a month to work his way through the kingdom. He spent time listening to the people his loved, and built trust by communicating with them.

When Diamante became king, he made the required fall tours. But his heart wasn't in it, and many people saw his insincerity. He wasn't interested in the details of government and even less in the people's opinions.

Diamante did spend several nights in many towns, as his father had done, but they were full of entertainment and late night parties. He often slept past noon the next day. He didn't listen very much and he learned very little.

This is not to say that King Diamante did not like to travel about the country. Throughout the year, he and his entourage took part in tournaments, concerts, and banquets, usually in the wealthiest cities and attended by glamorous Saggezzans and foreigners. Diamante and his hangers-on rolled through the countryside, hosting parties and competitions, enjoying the attention of the people. They loved being seen in expensive clothes and riding on the finest imported horses. They attended theaters with beautiful young women and laughed and danced until dawn.

During his fourth year as king, Diamante decided to break with tradition. Instead of touring the country after the harvest was brought in, he announced that he would visit the towns at various times throughout the year, whenever some event happened to bring him there.

This was not against the law, which required only that he visit each of the principal towns every year. Still, many Saggezzans thought that it was deeply inconsiderate. A royal visit during another event created crowds and distractions. It took the attention off the original event, which was often a local tradition, and focused it on Diamante. Of course, this is exactly what the young king wanted, but enough people resented it to cause grumbling. The month after the harvest was usually a holiday time for Saggezzans, when people had time to prepare for and participate in a royal visit. His visits at other times during the year interrupted work and harvest schedules, and many people found it difficult to be involved.

Diamante was a spectacular public figure: tall, handsome, and fashionably dressed. He waved and smiled at the townspeople during his grand entrances but did not eat with them or visit their homes or businesses. Local celebrities and wealthy citizens attended or hosted banquets held in his honor, and beautiful young women from the town were always invited to his parties.

Finally, people became frustrated enough to complain. The Saggezzan parliament had representatives from all the major towns. Early in the year, Diamante announced that he would be organizing a horse race in one prominent town during the spring planting, and that he would consider his attendance the royal visit to that place for the year. The citizens of the town felt disrespected, and they grumbled so much about it that their representative in Parliament spoke up during the assembly.

"We treasure his Highness and welcome any opportunity to show him our hospitality," he began, "But we could better attend to him—and perhaps he to us—if he would grace us with his presence during the autumn holidays, as his father did." The members of parliament nodded their heads and mumbled their approval.

A short time later, Diamante gave one of the port cities ten days notice that he was coming, and that this would be considered his required annual visit. The town council was puzzled as to what should prompt so sudden a visit so early in the year, and they pressed the royal messenger.

"The King has learned that the princess of Anatolia is on board one of that country's merchant vessels, on her way home from a visit to the Island of Regno. The King has always wished to meet her, and he has arranged to do so when she docks here. I am to organize a banquet and tournament in her honor. Since the King will be here for several days, he asks that you accept this as his legal visit this year. He requests that you arrange for him to meet with your council during the morning after her departure."

The citizens were stunned. Diamante would be in their town for two days, but most of his time would be spent wooing a foreign princess. The town council felt the king had insulted them by only granting them a breakfast meeting, and only after he had dallied with his foreign princess.

By the end of the summer, members of parliament were openly complaining throughout the corridors and courtyards of Avigliana. They looked at the castle above and grumbled about the lack of respect Diamante showed for the traditions of Monte Saggezza. They heard the noise coming down from the new fairgrounds and missed the quiet beauty of the gardens and orchards. They were alarmed at the rate of government spending, the increasing foreign debt, and the wave of new taxes that were strangling Saggezzan merchants, farmers, and craftsmen.

As the Prime Minister, Count Jalous was the leader of the Parliament, and he did everything he could to stoke the anger and frustration growing in Avigliana. He was careful not to speak out against the king in public, but he did encourage a few younger members in parliament to propose a resolution demanding that the king return to the "pattern of his father, the good King Bonum." Jalous had suggested that particular phrase to them, knowing how it would irritate Diamante. Jalous himself played the part of the loyal public servant trying to ease the conflict and restore order. Behind the scenes, however, he fanned the flames and undermined Diamante's support in the government.

"Are you sure you want me to keep going? It's getting late."
"C'mon dad." I waited.
"Alright." Reluctance was still hanging on his voice.

Diamante didn't pay much attention to the growing criticism. He did have many admirers, mostly young people who frequented his fairgrounds. He kept on organizing expensive public events: athletic competitions, horse races, and festivals. He visited the towns haphazardly, staying irregular amounts of time and keeping unusual hours. He was always surrounded by friends, assistants, celebrities, and fans. The townspeople got no opportunity to share their lives with him or hear words of encouragement or wisdom from their king. He let his underlings settle any local disputes or problems that were brought to him. Although Diamante was constantly in the public eye, the gap between the king and the citizens grew, and they understood each other less and less.

CHAPTER 11

The kings of Monte Saggezza had another unique responsibility. Every summer the king journeyed alone across the Ferus Mountains to the high northern plains. Once there, he was to seek out the summer encampment of the king of Ferox and renew the ancient bond between the two peoples. The king went by himself to show Saggezzans that he was strong enough to lead, and to show the Feroxans that he came in trust and kinship.

This law had been honored for centuries. When a king felt that he no longer had the strength for the trip it was time to pass the crown. The summer before he died King Bonum had struggled enough in the high passes that he knew it would be his last journey north.

A few months after he became king, Diamante strapped the massive Sword of Ferox to his back and walked confidently out the gate of Castello di San Michele, up through the orchards and onto the lower slopes of the Ferus Range. A remarkable athlete, he had no trouble crossing the mountains, although the trip took four days of steep climbing over difficult trails through snow, ice, and rock. Cresting the final pass, Diamante could see rolling grasslands, cut by snowmelt rivers, swept by winds off the

Northern Sea. Eager to complete this task, he descended into the wild plains of Ferox.

During the summer months the Feroxans were constantly on the move, hunting bison and tending their herds of horses. The Feroxan caravans were easy to follow, with broad swaths of trampled grass and streams muddied with passing scores of horses. For three days, he followed these obvious tracks. On the fourth day, he came upon hundreds of men, women and children accompanied by perhaps a thousand mounted warriors, flying the Feroxan royal standard. They were camped along a broad, rocky river that wound across the plain down to the Northern Sea, shrouded in fog.

Diamante strode down a long slope toward the encampment. When he was almost two miles away, a detachment of Feroxan sentries galloped up and surrounded him. Confident as always, he proudly announced himself as the monarch of Monte Saggezza and demanded to be immediately taken to their king.

His arrival caused excitement but not confusion, as Saggezzan kings had been arriving every summer for centuries. In due order, he was brought into a large tent which served as the Feroxan royal hall. The Feroxan king was old, and he looked skeptically at Diamante.

"Where is my dear friend, my kinsman, King Bonum?"

Diamante was determined to establish his own authority in the eyes of the northerners. In response to the king's question he pulled out the Sword of Ferox.

In order for each new generation of kings to recognize each other, the two royal houses had exchanged heirlooms and handed them down from king to king. The Feroxans had given the House of Saggezza a sword. The Sword of Ferox, as it became known, was a huge, heavy, brutally sharp object. The steel had been blended with an exotic northern metal, and the blade was a dull, charcoal color. The hilt was thick and, other than the mark of the Feroxan royal house, there was no other adornment. It was a simple tool, made for fierce battles in cold, wild lands. By contrast, blades in Monte Saggezza were light and elegant, crafted to be as pleasing to the eye as they were useful in a fight. A Saggezzan king had once sneered that the Sword of Ferox would be more suitable for butchering hogs than for the nimble fencing his people were used to.

Holding it high so that everyone in the royal tent could see, Diamante announced, "My father has gone to be with his fathers. I am Diamante, king of Monte Saggezza."

The King of Ferox sighed and felt tired, realizing that his generation was coming to an end. He regarded the young man in front of him. The physical resemblance was obvious, but Diamante's arrogant manner was nothing like his pleasant memories of King Bonum's annual visits.

Still, he realized, the work of diplomacy must go on. He nodded to one of his knights, who brought him a chest and unlocked it. The king opened it and removed the small wooden box. This was the other heirloom, given to the Feroxans by the House of Saggezza. It was an ancient Saggezzan counting box, a device consisting of colored marbles and dividers that were used to calculate large numbers. As much as the dark, northern sword represented the Feroxans, so this clever tool of trade and commerce was an icon of Monte Saggezza's culture.

After the presentation of the heirlooms, formal introductions were made and a feast was prepared. Diamante met various lords and knights, and, while he was polite, he was not interested in Feroxan politics, so he paid no attention to their names, titles, or positions.

If Diamante had been watching, he might have noticed a great deal of tension among the Feroxan court. The king had lost his wife and sons to various natural causes, accidents, or battles. He was now a widower and his only surviving child was a daughter, named Nordvindia.

Nordvindia was a slender but strong young woman. Her long, brown hair was braided and she was dressed in the same leather riding clothes that the knights around her wore. She had been raised in the saddle and could ride and hunt as well as any Feroxan knight. Her greatest gifts, though, were in leadership. She had grown up in the courts, learning how to solve problems and manage resources. She put people at ease and chose her words very carefully.

As her father the king got older, the Feroxan court speculated about who would take his place. Without a surviving male heir, some Feroxan lords saw an opportunity to take the throne. There was no law against Ferox having a queen, but it had been a two hundred years since there had been one. It was a warrior society, and the knights scheming for the crown didn't consider a thin, quiet girl to be a serious rival. A succession fight was brewing.

Diamante was oblivious to all of this. After a week of difficult travel he enjoyed the plentiful feast that night of roast meat, ale, and mead. But the next day he was already bored and wondering how long he was obligated to stay. He noticed Nordvindia's beauty, but there were plenty of beautiful women waiting back in Saggezza, and he was eager to return as soon as possible.

Every summer, King Bonum had arrived in Ferox as a friend who genuinely cared about his northern cousins. He had eaten what they ate and lived among them for a week or more, sharing the routines of their life. Understanding and affection grew on both sides.

Diamante did not make a good impression on the Feroxans. He was arrogant and standoffish. He boasted about Monte Saggezza's wealth and accomplishments. He showed little interest in their lives or their king's concerns and challenges. After only two days of strained conversation, Diamante announced that he would be leaving the next morning. The Feroxans were glad to see him go.

The next few summers, Diamante obeyed Saggezzan law and made the journey north, but the novelty had worn off and he showed even less interest than he had on his first trip. It was an unpleasant chore for him, an interruption in his summer activities. He went north as quickly as possible, stayed for what he considered two boring nights, and left. Each visit was more uncomfortable and strained than the last. Ferox was holding its breath as their king got older, its people worried about the coming fight between various chieftains and Nordvindia. Diamante was too self-absorbed to notice. He gave no thought to how Feroxan politics and personalities could affect his own kingdom.

CHAPTER 12

As he began his fifth summer as king, Diamante became distracted. It had been a hard winter and a late spring. He had invited many foreign artists, athletes, and entertainers to visit Monte Saggezza that summer for the festivals and tournaments. He personally enjoyed overseeing the preparations and spent the first few weeks of summer riding around the country arranging the details. Also, the fairgrounds on the old gardens around the castle had become a major source of revenue for the king, and he was busy expanding their size and scope.

The middle of June came and went, with his advisors and members of Parliament reminding Diamante that he was required to make his journey north. He kept delaying with the excuse that the snow was still too deep to cross the higher passes. When the first of July came his cabinet was alarmed. The passes were as clear as they would get, and the king was still not crossing them. By this time his foreign guests had arrived and Diamante was busy every night hosting, feasting, and reveling. The royal advisors stressed to him that the round trip to Ferox normally took him at least ten days. When would he go? Diamante waved them off by promising to go after the next banquet or festival.

On the first of August his cabinet was in a panic. The weather in the Ferus Range was unpredictable. Snowstorms had been known to hit as early as September. If he didn't leave immediately, it might be too late to make the journey. They knew that if Diamante failed to obey this law he could lose his claim to the throne, as well as the continued protection of the Feroxans.

Count Jalous saw the opportunity he had been waiting for. Two years before, he had begun conspiring with Bayezid, the King of the Island of Regno, to find an excuse to take the throne from Diamante. Jalous set in motion a plan that he had hoped would do just that.

First, he sent a secret communication, encouraging Bayezid to sail his flagship as quickly as possible to Saggezza's main port. Bayezid grasped Jalous' strategy and set sail the next day. Jalous also arranged for the Regnian ambassador to appear at Castello di San Michele and request, on behalf of his sovereign, that Diamante meet with King Bayezid for important trade negotiations.

Thus, near the end of the first week of August—just as Diamante was reluctantly planning to depart for Ferox—the Regnian royal squadron dropped anchor in Monte Saggezza's main harbor.

Diamante was caught in Jalous' trap. If he didn't depart northward within the next week, he would insult the Feroxans and break the law of Monte Saggezza. On the other hand, he could not afford to ignore and neglect the King of Regno, his most powerful rival.

It would take three days, riding at full speed and changing horses in every town, for Diamante to travel from Castello di San Michele to Monte Saggezza's main port on the Southern coast. He was sure that he could quickly conclude business with the Regnians, gallop back and still make it through the passes before the end of summer. He and his entourage charged down the hill to Avigliana the next morning.

At a rapid pace and with long hours in the saddle, Diamante actually shaved half a day off the journey, arriving at noon on the third day. While he changed out of his dusty riding clothes and refreshed himself in the royal apartments, he sent a message to the Regnians asking for a meeting that very afternoon.

But Jalous and Bayezid had been conspiring to slow down the proceedings. The messenger returned to Diamante with news that, since they had not expected him to travel so swiftly, King Bayezid, Count Jalous and the mayor of the town were fox hunting in the countryside, and would not return until late tomorrow. They begged his pardon, and they looked forward to beginning negotiations the day after that.

The next two weeks maddened Diamante and frightened his advisors. King Bayezid and Count Jalous slowed the negotiations to a crawl with complicated protocols and contentious issues. They stalled during meetings and misplaced documents. Their translators took a long time to consider each sentence. King Bayezid came down with a bout of stomach flu and begged Diamante's pardon for two days while he recuperated. Day after day the proceedings dragged on.

Diamante couldn't abandon the process since a breakdown in negotiations could mean war. The Regnians were known to pay pirates to harass their rivals, thus avoiding direct confrontation. But if Diamante could not renegotiate the treaty, Bayezid might feel free to use his powerful navy to seize Saggezza merchant vessels or even raid her coastal towns. Admiral Constante had warned Diamante about these threats for years and begged him not to divert funds from Saggezzan forces in order to fund fairgrounds and festivals. Diamante's advisors argued far into every night: some urged Diamante to depart immediately for Ferox to fulfill his obligation before it was too late; others warned that breaking off discussions with Regno could cause Saggezza's first war in over sixty years.

Bayezid and Jalous stalled enough that Diamante's cabinet suspected their conspiracy, but not so much that they could prove it. The royal advisors knew that Jalous had aspirations to the throne, but Diamante's behavior as king had weakened him politically, and they dared not challenge Jalous in Parliament.

After two weeks of frustration, Bayezid and Diamante signed the treaty. Diamante galloped north with new horses waiting for him in every town. On the last day of August, he left Castello di San Michele and began climbing the foothills carrying the Sword of Ferox.

The Ferus Mountains were a jagged wall at the head of the valleys of Monte Saggezza. Glaciers tumbled down steep ravines, and summer mists rose from them and met the warm, wet air blowing up the valleys from the southern sea. Sometimes these hot and cold vapors combined over the high peaks to produce violent storms, with the ocean waters falling as deep snow on the upper ranges.

As Diamante neared the passes, he met the most powerful mountain storm that he had ever seen. Heavy thunderstorms at middle elevations turned into blowing and drifting snow above the timberline, which blocked the upper pass completely. On the first night of September he sat huddled and freezing in a cave, still on the Saggezzan side of the divide, the trail outside covered by chest-deep snow drifts. The storm blew through the night, and the next morning when Diamante looked outside he was unable to see more than a few yards through the flurries blowing sideways across the buried trail. There was no way to continue.

That summer he had alienated his own citizens by failing to visit them properly. He had broken law and faith with the Feroxans by being the first Saggezza king in centuries not to make a summer visit. He had played into the hands of Jalous and Bayezid. Although he refused to acknowledge it, even to himself in that frozen cave, he had failed as king.

A few days later Diamante came striding back, through the fairgrounds and into Castello di San Michele with his head held high. Whatever he felt, he showed no sign of failure or even concern. His advisors pointed out that it wasn't too late to make amends for his mistakes. Even though he had announced that his summer festivities would replace the traditional royal visits to the towns, the harvest season was just beginning and he could still change his mind. As to the meeting with the Feroxans, he could address the Parliament, admit his error and depart immediately for the lower passes at the western end of the Ferus Range. It would be a longer and more difficult journey, but it would demonstrate his sincerity. He might still reach the Feroxan camp or even the Feroxan capitol if their king had returned to it for the winter. Such a journey would show them and his own country how much he valued the Feroxan bond.

No matter how much his advisors reasoned, begged, and warned him, Diamante would have nothing of it. He would not admit fault, take advice, or make amends. He explained that he was the king, and the law and people must learn that he was building a new Monte Saggezza, which was not bound by ancient traditions.

I thought of my business. Had I run it into the ground by not listening to those around me who tried to give good advice? Were there those who tried to help that I just ignored and chalked it up to a stubborn, entrepreneurial spirit?

My dad wasn't slowing down. He kept right on going. He had warned me; now he wasn't quitting.

CHAPTER 13

In the end, Diamante's birthday party was his downfall.

When faced with criticism, Diamante's instinct was always to change the subject and promote himself in other ways. Thus, his reaction that fall was to plan birthday celebrations for himself and throw the country the greatest party it had ever known. He imagined that people would be grateful for the good times and think of him fondly. Admiral Constante and others warned him that this was both foolish and dangerous, but Diamante didn't see it that way. He argued that the nation's concerns would be set aside in the festivities.

Monte Saggezza had many concerns. The short summer had caused a small harvest, and taxes were higher to pay for all of the king's projects. Everyone, from the family farmer to the wealthiest merchant, saw their income shrinking. Despite the new treaty, King Bayezid of Regno was becoming more aggressive, paying pirates to seize Saggezzan merchant ships. Many Saggezzan merchants who had invested everything in a trading voyage were bankrupted. The culture was becoming vulgar. Diamante had failed to tour the country and listen to their concerns and then missed his trip north to secure their relationship with their Feroxan kin. It was clear to everyone that he had been too distracted to fulfill his responsibilities. Many, maybe even most, citizens felt like Monte Saggezza had lost its way since Diamante had become king. Count Jalous and his adversarial allies in Parliament encouraged this frustration with gossip and angry speeches.

When the people heard that, in the midst of a meager harvest and hard times, the nation would take a three day holiday to celebrate Diamante's birthday, many began to speak out openly against him. Citizens struggling to pay their taxes were outraged at the thought of spending them on fireworks and drunken revelry. Parliament was in an uproar, and town councils sent letters of grievance to the palace. Frustration erupted into warring words throughout the town squares, workshops, and homes.

During the next month Diamante was occupied with planning his celebrations across the country. He was ignorant, or unconcerned, about the reaction the party preparations were causing. Count Jalous, on the other hand, was very aware. He had waited a lifetime for this opportunity and wasn't going to miss it.

Jalous organized his coup. He sent secret messages to King Bayezid of Regno and struck a bargain that would make him King of Monte Saggezza. In return he would become Bayezid's vassal, swearing his loyalty and support. But Monte Saggezza would be his, and he would remake it, just as he had dreamed for years.

While Diamante fussed about the smallest details of his parties, Jalous conspired with supporters in Avigliana, across the country, and even inside Castello di San Michele. It was not hard to find people unhappy with Diamante, even among his own cabinet. Others were angry about the economy, taxes, and excessive public spending on fairs and festivals that attracted the lazy and lethargic. Some were offended by the erosion of Monte Saggezza's traditions and culture. A great many more were worried that the country was no longer safe after Diamante had stripped its defenses and abandoned the Feroxans who guarded their northern border. Whatever people's worries, Count Jalous promised solutions, and he offered some conspirators positions in exchange for their support. When the king's birthday celebration arrived, the trap was laid.

On the first night of the royal birthday celebrations, Diamante was in the fairgrounds below Castello di San Michele. All afternoon there had been free concerts, open air dramas, and a boxing match between the Saggezzan champion and a famous foreign challenger. As part of his gift free ale was served to all in attendance. The crowd was huge, drunk, and rowdy. Diamante was everywhere, hosting, greeting, and waving. Many party goers sang songs about him, although more mocked than praised him. After sundown, the largest fireworks display in Saggezzan history was launched from the castle walls. While it took place, Diamante and his entourage were on horseback, descending the road to Avigliana, where an all-night street festival was underway.

As the royal party rounded a bend in the road that passed through a grove of trees near the base of the mountain, a contingent of armed horsemen surrounded them. The guards with Diamante were confused, for the newcomers wore the armor and uniforms of an elite unit of the national military, but the road between the castle and Avigliana was normally patrolled by the royal guardsmen. The fireworks burst over them, lighting the faces of the soldiers. They looked hard and determined, and their weapons were drawn.

Another burst illuminated their leader, Monte Saggezza's highest ranking general. While his soldiers hung back, menacing with swords and lances, he brought his horse alongside the king's.

"General Medici," began Diamante, cautiously, "What is this?"

"Sire, you must come with me immediately. There is an urgent matter that needs your attention."

"What is this matter? Where do you want me to go?"

"It is best if we speak in private. The war council has been called, and is waiting in the Parliamentary Hall. I am to escort you there."

Diamante tried to sound unconcerned. "Ah, how convenient for all us. We are going into town ourselves. Ride ahead and tell the council I am on my way, and I'll join you there shortly."

"Sire, I am to escort you there. Personally." General Medici paused. "Without your guard." He turned to the four royal guards sitting nervously on their horses, "Your men may return to the palace. We mean you no harm, but we will escort the king from here." The guards looked nervously from one to another, weighing their options.

Diamante was arrogant, but he wasn't stupid. He realized that General Medici was seizing him, and that this was a coup. He suspected Jalous was behind it, but that was irrelevant at the moment. He was sure that if he went with these men, he would lose his crown and probably his life. As the fireworks burst overhead, their booms echoing through the forest and making sharp shadows through the trees, he knew he must act quickly and seize the initiative.

Diamante was a natural athlete and had excelled at fencing and boxing from boyhood. Saggezzan fencing often involved two blades, a long rapier in the primary hand and a light dagger in the other. The shorter blade was used to parry blows and for stabbing or slashing at the opponent's blind side. That's what Diamante did now.

Medici's horse was drawn up next to his, on Diamante's left, facing the opposite direction. He could see that the general's gaze alternated between Diamante's face, his right hand and the hilt of his rapier, wondering if the king would resist arrest. Diamante timed his move for the moment of darkness after a flash from the fireworks, and during the boom that followed a second later.

In one fluid motion his left hand drew his short sword and slashed it across the general's thigh, only a couple inches from his own. The general reacted by tensing his leg in the stirrup, which caused his horse to flinch, and looked down toward the pain near his saddle. That was exactly what Diamante had hoped for, as he twisted and brought his right fist across his body, punching Medici square in the face, instantly breaking his nose.

It happened so quickly, with the flashes of fireworks and noise from overhead, that no one else really understood what was going on. Men shouted and horses reared.

Diamante knew that there was no point in galloping off. He was on the narrow road between the castle and the town, and whichever way he rode, he would be trapped. Instead, he reared his horse and slid off the back. As the soldiers, guards, and members of his entourage shoved, fought, and shouted at each other, he rolled through the hooves into the underbrush beside the road. Before anyone realized what had happened, he had quickly crawled twenty yards into the forest. With the light and noise of the fireworks, it was as if he had disappeared.

Diamante had grown up on this mountain, hiding from his teachers, guards, and anyone trying to catch him for the mischief he had caused. He knew all its contours and hiding spots. More importantly, he knew every way in and out of the tunnels under Castello di San Michele.

CHAPTER 14

The bend in the road was crowded with Diamante's guards and friends and the two dozen soldiers General Medici had brought. The flashes from the fireworks lit the struggling soldiers and rearing horses, and everyone shouted to be heard over the noise of the explosions above.

It wasn't easy to sort out the confusion, and no one knew which way to go. General Medici was barking orders, realizing that he had to find the king quickly, and in the confusion two of Diamante's guards had wheeled their horses and raced back up the road toward the castle. Medici divided his force, sending a group down toward the bridge into town and another chasing the guards back up to the castle gates. He didn't know where to search for Diamante. He was sure that dismounting and wandering around the forest, with no clear idea of where to look, was a waste of time and manpower that he couldn't afford.

By the time anyone realized that he was gone, Diamante was more than a hundred yards into the dense pines, moving up and across the hill. By the time General Medici sent men toward the town and the castle, Diamante was almost a quarter mile away, where the pines gave way to a stand of hardwoods near a pile of boulders under a small cliff. The fireworks occasionally lit up the area, casting dark shadows under the trees. Diamante paid no attention since he knew where he was going and could easily find his way in the dark. In fact, he had done it so many times as a teenager that sneaking into or out of the castle had become second nature.

Diamante slipped through the oaks and up to the bottom of a little cliff. At its base a large boulder, the size of a small house, leaned against it. Diamante scrambled up it, across the top and lowered himself through a gap between the rock and the wall.

He dropped onto a small, sandy clearing, lit only by the moonlight coming through the opening over his head. In front of him was a rough passage, about chest high, running slightly upward into the cliff. Diamante squatted to enter it. Before he did, he grabbed an unlit torch and a flint from a wooden box on the floor. For centuries teenagers had probably been using this passage to sneak in or out. The box of torches had been here when he was a boy and first discovered it. He had always replaced what he had used, and it appeared that another generation of teens was using it as well to get into mischief.

Diamante crawled a couple hundred yards up the slope to an opening with faint firelight coming through it. He paused and looked through. It was a large space, a sort of warehouse. There were barrels and crates everywhere, and a few oil lamps hung overhead. Seeing no one, he slid from the opening between two large barrels into the storeroom.

The hill under the castle was full of caves and passages. They served as storage and refuge in times of war. With space being so limited in the mountaintop fortress, the caves were also used for many of the ordinary functions that supported castle life. There were bakeries and breweries, forges, stables for animals during winter and plenty of storerooms like this one. There were many shafts like the one he had crawled through which allowed ventilation, or escape in times of war, but few people knew them all like he did.

Diamante took a moment to consider what he should do. Clearly someone—he suspected Jalous—was stealing the crown and had organized forces to do so. Since anyone might be a conspirator, he could trust no one. But that left few options. He could not defeat Jalous alone. He had no money and was too well recognized to sneak out of Monte Saggezza.

He was sure that he still had some friends. At least he had friends who had been happy to spend his money during good times. He thought of one friend whom he felt was trustworthy, if he could only get there. It would be a two days ride away. Once safely hidden in his friend's villa, he could plan his next moves.

The more he considered it, he realized that there were three things he needed: a horse, money, and the Sword of Ferox, the symbol of his office. If he had any hope of reclaiming the throne, he would need all three.

He could easily steal a horse from the stables, or one tied up in the fairgrounds. The money and the Sword would be more difficult. The Sword was kept in his private chambers, high in the castle towers. He also kept a considerable stash of gold coins there. The challenge would be getting there before Jalous did. He must not let the Sword fall into his enemy's hands. It occurred to Diamante that Jalous might already have gone to his rooms and taken it. Well, he shrugged to himself, there was no way to know without trying.

Diamante began working his way up through the underground complex. With the fireworks and the festival there were not many people working down there that evening, but he knew some areas were busy day and night, all year, like the bakeries. He skirted around these sections, taking an indirect route through rarely used passages. He had spent his boyhood down here, sneaking treats and playing pranks. He smiled wryly to think that it had finally been worth it.

As he approached the lower levels of the castle, it became harder to hide. These areas were barracks, armories, and stables, and the last thing he wanted to do right now was encounter any guards or soldiers. Diamante slowed down, waiting at each corner until a passerby had moved on and skirted around groups that were talking or distracted. He had worked his way through these areas hundreds of times, but back then the worst thing that might happen to him if caught was a scolding. This time the stakes were much higher.

It took an hour of creeping through a butler's pantry, the ladies' baths and a dry water shaft leading to an unused cistern, but eventually he reached the stairs leading up to the royal apartments. As he crept into the circular stairwell he could hear shouting from up above. He had no idea if they were loyalists or conspirators, but he was out of options. He couldn't go back down the way he came and hide in a pantry forever. He realized that he might have to fight his way into the apartment and then, for the second time that night, escape back into the underground during the confusion afterward. He drew his sword and his dagger and began circling up the stairs.

As he went, the shouting got louder and more angry, and then he heard the unmistakable sound of combat, as steel clanged and bodies tangled. Rounding the top, he cautiously looked past the corner to the door of the royal apartment. Four soldiers, wearing the uniforms of General Medici's force, lay dead on the threshold. Diamante gripped his blades and crept through the open door.

Inside were three traitors, held captive by a handful of Admiral Constante's marines. They turned on Diamante, weapons drawn, but a voice commanded them to hold. Constante himself had sunk onto the sofa, bleeding profusely from a large gash in his neck.

"Sire, we came as soon as we heard what Jalous was doing. He has supporters everywhere. The government, the military—even businessmen."

Diamante was, perhaps for the first time in his life, grateful for the admiral. Constante had given his life defending his crown, when Diamante had done nothing but frustrate the old man. "Admiral, you must rest." He ordered two of the marines to send for a surgeon.

"Your highness," Constante continued, struggling to speak with the blood flowing from his neck, "I have protected the sword."

Diamante sat next to Constante on the couch.

"The Sword of Ferox?" Diamante leaned in. "Where is it?"

"It must stay hidden. Without it Jalous will never be legitimate. The House of Saggezza must reclaim the throne..."

"Admiral, please, where have you hidden it?"

Constante grabbed Diamante's tunic and pulled him in close to whisper in his ear. "Don Verde..."

"The Master Gardener?" Diamante was puzzled. He hadn't thought of him in a long while.

"Your father, Verde...and I...we were all boys together. He can be trusted. Wait until you are ready."

With that, Constante took his last breath and slumped into Diamantes' arms.

At that moment, General Medici marched through the doorway with a company of men behind him.

I think I could actually see the pain in my dad's eyes. Like he knew the general or the gardener personally. Maybe they were like some of his former business partners. He didn't elaborate, and just kept going.

I thought of Brandon and Todd and wondered would they risk it all for me. They had already in a sense.

CHAPTER 15

After that, things moved very quickly for Diamante. The moment he saw Medici, he sprung from the couch like a scared cat. He drew his sword and lunged toward General Medici.

General Medici, his thigh bleeding through a field bandage, sent Diamante sprawling across the room with the back of a gauntleted hand. Diamante crashed into a cabinet, wine bottles and goblets falling over his head. He regained his footing and slashed his sword about him like a mad man. With his enemies surrounding him he lunged once more for General Medici, falling short. Before he could respond, Medici stood on Diamantes' sword and kicked him hard in the stomach, then in the head. Diamante's head began to swim, his memory and abilities fading fast. Before he could move again, a company of soldiers was on top of him.

The next thing that he did remember was being locked in a prison wagon, bumping along a dark road somewhere. He hurt everywhere, with fresh bruises and open wounds all over his body. His head was throbbing and his mouth tasted like some sort of medicine or drug had been poured into it. He wondered where he was and where he was going, but there was no one to ask. He was kept in wagons and cells. His food was left for him and his bucket taken by unspeaking guards. When he was moved outdoors a black hood was placed over his head.

After a few days he was led, hooded, onto a ship. The sounds, smells and movement left no doubt, and it was clear that he was being taken down into the hold below the waterline. He was chained to a bulkhead and his hood was removed. Diamante had no idea where he was headed, except that it was far away from Monte Saggezza.

Overnight, Count Jalous became king. His conspirators had moved quickly and eliminated any potential opposition. Jalous was backed by Regnian forces that had slipped into the country in small groups, disguised as merchants. They had brought lots of Regnian gold, which helped win over more rivals than by using force.

Over the next few months Jalous relished the role that he had dreamed about and schemed for. He told himself, and anyone that would listen, that he had taken the crown to make Monte Saggezza a more glorious country. King Bonum had ruled with a light, fatherly touch. Diamante had squandered the nation's wealth on his own pleasures, ignoring justice and the responsibilities of government. Jalous' approach was something no Saggezzan had foreseen or desired: he managed every aspect of the kingdom's life. No detail was too small, nor any citizen too unimportant to escape his regulations. There were rules about how cheese should be made and sold. The manufacture of everything from cloth to clocks was monitored by government inspectors, to make certain that it complied with royal objectives that no one understood. These objectives never seemed to be written down anywhere so people could figure them out. Jalous issued rules about how people could build their houses, what students should learn in school, and how people should treat their horses. He didn't aspire to lead the country to glory, but to remake it according to his own glorious imagination, and by the force of his own rather inglorious power. Within months, Saggezzans realized that the vain neglect of Diamante had been replaced by the vain dictatorship of Jalous.

There were Regnians everywhere. In return for the crown, Jalous had pledged loyalty to King Bayezid, but Bayezid cared nothing for Jalous' affection or loyalty: it was the wealth of Monte Saggezza that he really wanted. Few people realized, at first, that many of the regulations that came from Jalous' army of government workers actually gave an advantage to Regno. Saggezza craftsmen and their ingenious works had been considered the best in the world. The new rules forced them to make things in ways and for prices that were no better, if not worse, than Regnian products. The ports of Monte Saggezza had always been busy loading ships to take the bounties of the country to distant lands, coming back full of gold and precious gems. By the end of the first year of Jalous' reign the ships seemed to be always unloading lower quality Regnian products and sailing away with the country's wealth. Regnian merchants and advisors were always accompanied by armed "assistants."

The following summer, the elderly Count Jalous went north, making a show of complying with the royal responsibilities. But he didn't go alone, instead taking a large armed entourage. He also went without the Sword of Ferox, which his servants had searched for endlessly. Jalous hated the idea of a solitary journey over the Ferus Range, and knew that he didn't have the ability to survive such an ordeal anyway. So, like he had with everything else, he made new rules. He took the lower, easier passes far to the west and his little troop wandered slowly, carefully across the Feroxan plain.

When he finally did stumble upon the Feroxan royal camp, it was an odd and awkward meeting. Jalous had come north without the heirloom to prove that he was the rightful king, and with an armed escort, in violation of the treaty and bonds of friendship.

Strangely, the King of Ferox did not challenge Jalous on these points. As well, he seemed nervous, and was clearly not expecting a Saggezzan delegation of any kind to show up that summer. Even more strange, he never asked Jalous to see the Sword of Ferox, nor did he offer to show the Counting Box of Saggezza. Instead, he ordered a feast for the Saggezzans with large amounts of powerful Feroxan ale, and everyone forgot about protocols and treaties.

The truth was that the Feroxan king didn't have the heirloom counting box. During the previous winter the king of Ferox had died. For years various northern lords had been planning to contest the succession when that happened. The king who welcomed Jalous that summer was the winner of that fight, and most of his rivals were dead.

The princess Nordvindia had been chased out. There was nothing in Feroxan law that prevented her from inheriting the crown, but just because it was allowed didn't mean that it was acceptable. There were too many warlike men that wanted it too badly. Her cousin, the sonless king's nephew, began eliminating his rivals the same night that he seized power. The princess rode out of the camp two hours before dawn that fateful night, and when the sun rose she saw the foothills of the Ferus Mountains rising above the high, cold plains.

She had with her a young knight who had honorably served her father, an old Feroxan trader who had served as her tutor, and two horses loaded with baggage. She had a few days supplies of food, a change of clothes, a few weapons, and several bags of trade goods. The foothills on the northern side of the Ferus Range had always been rich in silver, and nuggets of gold tumbled down from the mountains through the rocky river beds that wound across the windblown grasslands. Eventually those rivers ran down to the North Sea, between which yielded precious amber and ivory. For centuries Feroxan traders had carried these items across the mountains to Saggezzan marketplaces under protection of the treaty with the kings of Monte Saggezza. Now, Nordvindia hoped, they would buy her freedom and a new life in the lowlands.

She had also grabbed one other item from her father's tent: the Saggezzan Counting Box, that identified her father —and now her—as the rightful ruler of Ferox to the rightful ruler of Monte Saggezza.

CHAPTER 16

A week later Nordvindia and her two companions had crossed the mountains over a remote southern pass that Feroxan traders had used for centuries. She was amazed by the green Saggezzan valleys. She had only known the vast spaces of Ferox. In winter the snow blew down from the cold sea, and in summer the high grasses moved in waves, but the wind always blew across rolling plains. It was an unconsidered constant in her life. Now she marveled at the intimacy of the valleys, with vineyards tucked into dales along little rivers, and villages perched like beehives on top of little hills.

Her older companion had been this way many times. His name was Jakob, and many in his clan engaged in trade with Saggezza and Ferox's other neighbors. His wife had died when they were young, leaving him childless, and he had spent much of his life traveling through Saggezza and other countries. Even though he was unmistakably Feroxan, he spoke the Saggezzan language and understood their customs well enough to conduct business.

Her younger companion was barely a Feroxan knight, having earned his lance and the right to ride into battle only a few months earlier. His name was Ragnar, he was her cousin and he had adored her growing up. When it became clear that she had to flee, Ragnar had appointed himself her protector. These lowland valleys were just as strange to him, but he eyed them suspiciously, ready to defend her from any danger.

They rode their shaggy, northern horses down cobbled roads and through orderly market towns with red-tiled roofs. Monte Saggezza was a merchant country and its people were used to seeing foreigners. Feroxans were the rarest of traders, but not unheard of. Under normal circumstances some Saggezzans might have struck up a conversation or asked about their business. But circumstances in Monte Saggezza were not normal.

For one thing, there were Regnians everywhere. Nordvindia had never seen a Regnian and had no idea how to tell one from a Saggezza. They all looked and sounded strange to her. But the Saggezzans noticed her and her companions and were alarmed. The Regnians never traveled alone or in parties of two or three, as merchants might. They rode about in groups that numbered in the dozens, almost like military units. They weren't visibly armed, but their behavior seemed vaguely menacing.

The Feroxans had lived in open spaces their whole lives. On their first night in a cultivated valley, Nordvindia and Ragnar were ready to hunt and make camp somewhere along the road. Jakob tried to explain that this wasn't done in Monte Saggezza. The princess and the young knight struggled to understand why it wasn't. This whole country was strange to them, but they trusted Jakob's experience and agreed to spend money to stay in something called an "inn."

As they approached a roadside village, Jakob coached them in how to behave. His clan had done business for generations in Saggezza, and his family name would be useful in establishing contacts. Nordvindia and Ragnar, however, were from the ousted royal clan, and must change their names. Ordinary Saggezzans would be unlikely to know about the political turmoil in Ferox, but word could quickly travel to unfriendly ears. He would introduce them as his kinfolk, along to learn the family business. The princess agreed, but pleaded to hold onto some shred of her identity.

"What would my name be, in the Saggezzan language?"

Jakob took a bit to work it out in his head, before answering. "Saggezzans would call our *nord vind* the *aquilo*." He thought about it. "For a woman's name, they might say *aquila*."

"Aquila? Aquila." She listened to herself, considering it, then shrugged. "So I shall be Aquila, an apprentice trader."

That night, Aquila had her first encounter with Saggezzan culture. She didn't understand a word that was said, but she was fascinated by the whole process: Jakob negotiating, how they were assigned rooms, the tavern on the ground floor where meals were served, and other travelers drinking ale, laughing and arguing about topics she couldn't follow.

The next day, they continued on to a larger town and another inn. Along the way, Jakob taught Aquila and Ragnar about Saggezza, about the business of importing and exporting trade goods, and their first words of the Saggezzan language. The former princess kept interrupting with questions about everything she saw or didn't understand. If she was to have a new life, she was determined to make a success of it.

They were in no particular hurry. They had a small fortune in silver and other valuables, and nowhere they had to be. They worked their way slowly along the roads through the valleys, in the general direction of La Spezia, the country's largest seaport. Jakob had been there many times and knew it to be a busy place with lots of foreigners coming, going and staying. It was a perfect place for them to start over. Aquila had no better idea, and trusted Jakob's judgment anyway. Ragnar was determined to go wherever his royal cousin went and keep her from harm.

They talked about their options. Their small fortune would last a while, maybe even a few years, but not forever. Unless they returned to Ferox on the hope of political change there, they must invest in some business that would provide for their future. Jakob explained various ways that they could import and export goods in a busy seaport, and the ways they could make or lose money doing so.

As they worked their way to the coast, Jakob listened to the gossip and arguments in the taverns. Most of it was about politics, and most of it was bad. Monte Saggezza was becoming a vassal state, virtually a colony of Regno, and the tavern-goers were angry. Jalous was a petty tyrant. On every issue that mattered, he took his instructions from the Regnians. Jalous, who had longed to take orders from no one, had to content himself with managing the most trivial aspects of his citizens' lives. Everything was regulated and government officials meddled in every family, business, and village. The citizens were angry and complained that they didn't recognize their own country after the incompetence of Diamante and the puppet leadership of Jalous. As the evening wore down, the Saggezzans would raise their final pints and toast the good old days of King Bonum.

They had traded their shaggy Feroxan horses for sleek mounts at the first market town they had passed. As they rode each morning, Jakob related the previous night's tavern talk. Of course Aquila and Ragnar had never known the old Monte Saggezza, but the three talked about how the current state of affairs should affect their plans.

They arrived in the port city of La Spezia almost seven weeks after they fled the Feroxan camp. They took rooms at an inn near the docks, and Jakob made some small but shrewd deals with some of his contacts there. He was a good teacher, and Aquila and Ragnar were quick learners. They invested their money wisely and multiplied it quickly. Like immigrants in so many countries they adapted, worked hard, and built a successful new life.

CHAPTER 17

Twelve years passed by and Monte Saggezza had changed. Under King Bonum it had been a prosperous land of ingenious craftsmen and shrewd merchants that spent less than they earned. Diamante had made it a less serious place, spending the nations' wealth on public entertainment and spectacles. Since Jalous' coup the country had become almost a colony of the Regnian Empire.

The Emperor of Regno set the prices for Saggezza goods, and craftsmen barely made a living mass producing cheap products, which the Regnians sold across their empire for huge profits. There were endless regulations on Saggezza farmers, which made it impossible for them to compete with the grain, wine, and other products, which Regno imported from its other colonies. Young Saggezzans had fewer opportunities, and more left the country to find work in other parts of the empire or enlisted in the Regnian military. The ancient bond with Ferox was broken. With the Sword and Counting Box both missing, the usurpers on both thrones ignored each other. Monte Saggezza became poorer and the people more disconnected from their leaders.

Despite the general condition of things, Aquila and her companions had done well. There were always ways to make a profit on the import and export of goods. They invested in shipping, bought from and sold to the international merchants that came and went from the port, and purchased an inn near the docks. Although they couldn't hide their northern features or accents, no one suspected that the owner of The North Wind, the city's largest inn, was the exiled princess of Ferox.

It was a busy night in the common room. Three large ships had put into port yesterday and hundreds of travelers from around the world had disembarked in search of lodging. There were few rooms available, as hundreds of Saggezza young men, recruited as laborers in other Regnian colonies, waited to board company ships the next day. The North Wind was packed and Aquila was having kitchen problems. Half the fish she had ordered from the market that morning had arrived with a rotten smell, one of her ale casks had a pressure leak, and her head chef had quit the day before to work for her rival down the street. Service was slow, the menu limited, and the ale was flat. She had heard complaints in six languages in the last hour.

She stood at the head of one long table, trying to calm a rowdy bunch of Regnian merchants who were refusing to pay for their meals after waiting an hour to be served. As she haggled, her eye was caught by a tall man sitting at the far end of the table that looked down in embarrassment at his companions' behavior. He looked familiar to her, but she couldn't remember where she had seen him before. After twelve years of doing business with travelers in a busy port, she didn't think too long about it. She negotiated a solution with the unhappy customers and moved on to the next problem.

As the evening wound down and the tavern gradually emptied, she noticed the tall man again. He sat in the back, alone with cup of hot, spiced wine. He was fiddling with a counting box. Aquila had become an expert with a box, doing calculations throughout the day with one hand and recording them in her ledgers with another, as quick as thought. The stranger was more deliberate, reflecting on each move of the pieces. He had no papers to work from or write his results onto. He just sat, thinking and figuring something out with the box. After a few minutes he finished his cup, left a tip for the server, and went upstairs to his room.

The next night was less hectic at The North Wind. Aquila had hired a new chef, replaced the bad ale cask, and made it clear to the fish vendor that he would regret the day he ever unloaded his rotten inventory on her again. While the inn still had no vacancy, she was able to relax and chat with some of her customers.

She saw the tall, quiet man again, but the grain merchants he had been sitting with last night had checked out. Tonight he sat at a common table with a smattering of other single travelers, chatting pleasantly. Again, she knew that she knew him from somewhere, but paid no particular attention. The North Wind had well over a hundred guests tonight and dozens of them had probably stayed here at some point in the past. She assumed he must have been a guest at some point over the last decade. Later, as the last quests lingered before going upstairs for the night, she again saw him making some sort of slow, silent calculations with his counting box.

The same thing happened each day for a week. He left the inn early for whatever business had brought him to the city. In the evenings he ate in the common room at any table with an empty seat, and ended his day by reflectively lingering over his counting box. Though she had had thousands of guests and had done business with thousands of merchants over the years, there was something about this particular man, which bothered her. The more she thought about it, she didn't think that she knew him as former guest or colleague. At times she glanced across the room and caught him staring at her, as if he too was trying to connect her to some distant memory, but both of them looked quickly away.

His stride gave her the context she needed. It was late afternoon and she was in front of The North Wind, talking to Ragnar. He had been away on business for a few weeks, and had returned with a wagon load of goods for export. As workers unloaded the wagon into their warehouse next to the inn, she glanced up the street which rose uphill away from the harbor. Out of the corner of her eye she caught site of the tall stranger striding down toward the inn. He walked with a long, loping confidence, his arms swinging carelessly. In an instant she knew that she had seen that self-assured stride, coming down an open, grassy slope, not here in the confined streets of the port. She interrupted Ragnar and pointed up the road.

"That man, the tall one in the blue tunic, coming past the butcher's shop. Does he seem familiar to you?"

Ragnar watched the man approach. He stared, squinted, looked away, and looked back again. Confusion gave way to wonder, then concern.

"My lady, I have seen that man before. I was a boy, and I remember the day well. My father and brothers let me ride out of the camp to watch him approach. It was the first time I had ridden with the men, and the first time I had ever seen a foreigner."

It came back to Aquila as well. She remembered the scouts galloping into camp, the urgent orders her father barked, the knights galloping out with pennants on their lances. Her father wouldn't allow her to ride out with them, but she did run to the edge of the camp and watched them escort him in.

The question was, what was he doing here? If she recognized him, might he know who she really was? If so, was she in any danger?

CHAPTER 18

Although he was part owner, Jakob didn't spend much time at The North Wind. The three Feroxan exiles were partners in several businesses and Jakob spent most of his time across the harbor in their warehouse near the marketplace. After getting a message from Aquila, he hurried right over. After they filled him in, he sat drinking in the common room, waiting for the stranger to come in. Although it might not have occurred to him, once it was pointed out, he made the same connection that they did. Now the three of them sat in Aquila's office and debated their next move.

They realized that if they recognized him, others would as well. It was only a matter of time before trouble arose, and they didn't want to be in the way when it did. It was decided that Aquila would approach their guest to discover what he was doing in their inn. Ragnar, Jakob and a few of their men would be ready in case things went badly.

The tall stranger had arrived back to the inn around nightfall and went to his room for a few hours. As was his habit, he came down in the middle of the evening, took an open seat at a common table, and made small talk with those around him while they ate. As the crowd gradually retired and the hall emptied, he ordered a cup of hot, spiced wine and sat near the fire. He reached into his bag, pulled out his counting box, and quietly began fiddling with it.

Jakob drank some ale in the opposite corner and Ragnar was seated at the bar. Aquila approached the stranger and asked if she might take a seat.

The stranger looked at her a long time without answering, then smiled and gestured to the chair across the table. Aquila waved over one of her servers who brought two fresh cups of spiced wine. The stranger began to protest that he didn't need a new drink, but Aquila dismissed him with a wave. "On the house," she smiled.

As if she was merely curious, Aquila asked him where he was from and what he was doing in town. He answered politely that he had grown up in Monte Saggezza, but had worked abroad for many years. He had just returned and was staying at the inn while he looked for permanent work.

"And what about you," he asked. "You look like someone from a Northern country. From your accent, I would say... Ferox?" He smiled enigmatically.

Aquila leaned forward and spoke in a low voice, "You can tell I am Feroxan because, I think, because you have been there yourself." She leaned even further, and hissed, "Am I right?" The stranger tried to hold her gaze but looked down at his counting box after a moment.

Aquila continued. "My friends and I," she pointed a thumb over her shoulder in the direction of Jakob and Ragnar, "remember you. Maybe you remember me, maybe not. All of that was another life, I think for you as well as us. We want to know what you are doing in our inn. Have you come to cause trouble for us? Or will it just follow you here?"

A long time went by. The stranger didn't look up. "I do remember you. I saw you staring at me this week. At first I couldn't put it together, who you were. But I haven't known too many Feroxans. It came to me. I do wish I could remember your name."

Aquila glanced around the near-empty room to make sure no one overhear. Even so, her voice was a hostile whisper. "But I remember yours, King Diamante. Or shall I just say Diamante?"

The pause was so long that Aquila glanced at Jakob and shrugged. Then the man nodded slowly and met her eyes with a wry half-smile. "I haven't heard anyone call me by that name in almost thirteen years. And you are correct, there is no longer a title in front of that name. I assume you are also no longer the princess of Ferox?"

"I am no longer a princess. I am a businesswoman. My name is Aquila."

"Ah, of course," said Diamante. "I should have figured it out. The North Wind, Aquila. Your name was," he looked up, trying to recall the Feroxan language, "Nordvindia? Princess Nordvindia, wasn't it?"

Aquila leaned back and eyed him suspiciously. "Why are you here, my lord? You disappeared when Jalous took the throne. This country is full of theories about what happened to you. Most now believe that you're dead. Yet here you are, in my inn, of all places. What does it mean?"

"It doesn't mean anything. I had to stay somewhere. This was recommended as the best inn in La Spezia. Wherever I go there is a chance I will be recognized. It just happened to be you."

Aquila leaned and jabbed a finger at him. "We have forgotten Ferox. It has forgotten us," she hissed, "We want it all to stay forgotten. If you have come to make trouble for me and my friends then get out now."

"Does it ever stay forgotten?" asked Diamante. "I can't forget who I was. Sometimes I wish I could." He looked down and fiddled with his counting box.

Aquila sat back and watched him. "What happened to you? Where have you been?"

Diamante laughed. "I'll tell you my story if you tell me yours. As odd as mine might be, I can't imagine how a northern warrior-queen became an inn keeper next to a wharf in La Spezia."

Diamante seemed relaxed and unthreatening, and Aquila was curious. But she knew that if the Saggezza or Regnian authorities caught the former king in her inn it would be the end of The North Wind. She suggested they continue their talk in her private office.

It was a functional room, with a warm fire and deep armchairs around the hearth. She invited Jakob and Ragnar to join them, since they had as much to lose from any trouble that might follow Diamante as she did. The four of them got comfortable with warm drinks and a plate of snacks were brought in.

Aquila introduced her companions and began by telling Diamante about the coup in Ferox. She described their flight over the mountains, their arrival in the port and gave a brief overview of their business career since then.

Diamante was interested and surprised. He asked a few questions and shook his head, smiling at the strange journey that had changed their lives so much.

Aquila crossed her arms and settled back. "Now it's your turn," she said.

Diamante sipped his wine, nodded, and began.

"*Alright, that's enough for now plus I'm not sure I know how it goes anymore.*"

"*What? You've got to be kidding me. No way dad!*" *I had kind of startled myself. I usually wasn't that demanding or forward with my dad.* "*Hey I know, let's look for it in the garage.*" *I could have used a breath of fresh air and I knew he couldn't resist the opportunity to go out for a smoke. We made our way out to the garage with a bunch of his grumbling and thanks to my mother, who labeled everything, we were able to find the story he wrote and kept.*

"*There, now you've the got notes.*"

He took the papers and pushed his cigarette out in an old seven up can. "*Hmmm*" *he shook his head and went back in the house. Flipping through the pages he found his place and with out my prodding he started back up.*

CHAPTER 19

Thirteen years ago, I threw myself the biggest birthday party Monte Saggezza had ever seen. It was a stupid, selfish thing to do. The people had resented me for a long time, and the party only made it worse. It also gave my enemies the perfect opportunity to remove me from the throne.

I was in Castello di San Michele, the royal castle outside the capitol of Avigliana. I had arranged for a massive fireworks show over the castle that evening. Count Jalous—he was prime minister back then—had his men try to seize me during the show, while everyone was distracted. I managed to escape them, but had no clear idea where to go. I realized that Jalous meant to seize the crown. I could not abide the thought of him holding it forever.

As you know, one of the ancient heirlooms of the Saggezzan monarchy is the Sword of Ferox. It was given in friendship to the first king of Monte Saggezza to acknowledge the kinship between our peoples. More than any other item, its possession has always been a symbol of rightful power in our country. That night, during Jalous' coup, I resolved that he would never take the Sword.

I crept back into the castle through little known ways, into my royal chambers where the sword was kept.

Unfortunately, I was too late. I arrived only in time for my most faithful advisor to die in my arms. He had been my father's best friend, and was more loyal to this country than I was. He died defending the Sword, which he had hidden. Before I could learn where it was, Jalous' men entered. They struck me on the back of my head, and I passed out.

I don't remember much about the next couple of days. They gave me a foul medicine that clouded my mind and confused my senses. They put a hood over my head so I could see nothing. I was kept in a series of rooms, cold and injured. I was transported in the back of a wagon, but I only know this by the sounds and smells. I fell in and out of a stupor. I lost track of time.

After some days I was carried onto a ship like a sack of grain. I was chained in the hold, behind crates and barrels of cargo. They finally removed the hood, but I had no idea what ship it was or where it was going. I knew it was Regnian by the inscriptions on the barrels and the speech of the crew. But other than the most basic interactions with the guards who brought me food, I had no contact with anyone. There was no window, and I had no idea which direction we traveled. I did manage to scratch a mark for each night. I could see slivers of light through the decking overhead and counted forty-two sundowns on that ship. I never left the hold, and my injuries never healed properly. My body and my mind grew sick. I despaired.

On the forty-third day we put into port. I was dragged from the hold, for I could barely walk. When I came on deck my eyes burned from seeing daylight, but I got my first sight of the land we had come to. It was a hot, dry country of steep hills covered with brown grasses and prickly plants. We were tied up at a pier in a busy harbor, but many of the ships were of a design I had never seen before and flying colors that were strange to me. I was loaded into a cart and driven into the center of the city. Everything was foreign to my eyes. The buildings were of clay bricks, but brightly painted. The people were of many colors, and I could not understand their languages. I was taken to a crowded market square, full of strong smells and loud noises. I was put into a large, open-air cage with dozens of other unfortunate souls that looked as desperate as I did.

We were given a surprising amount food and drink for a few days and encouraged to walk about to regain our strength. Although I did not understand our captors, I found some common languages with other prisoners, and they were able to interpret for me. We were to make ourselves as presentable as possible before we were to be sold as slaves in a few days. I considered not cooperating, but I realized that if I was to become a slave I was better off being a valuable one. I ate everything available and exercised as best as I could.

The auction was four days later. I had heard of such things, but of course had never seen it with my own eyes. It was sad and humiliating, and I didn't understand what was happening. There was a crowd around our cage. We were jostled and grabbed by the guards as foreigners pointed and shouted at us. All I knew was that after about an hour I was shackled to perhaps a dozen other prisoners and we were marched out of the city.

We walked at spear-point over a dirty, rocky road for another week. By the time we arrived our feet were bleeding and our skin was burned from the blazing sun. I cursed the sun, which I had missed for all those days on the ship. If I had only known that I would not see it again for more than ten years I would have felt more affection for it.

We had come to a mine in a rocky valley. Actually it was a whole series of mines, connected by a crude but enormous series of tunnels. Outside the entrance was a fortress, full of soldiers. They guarded not only the slaves, but the mines themselves and what they produced. For these mines, remote and unknown, were a great source of wealth to the monarch of that country. Veins of gold and precious stones lay in the bowels of those hills. Fresh slaves and soldiers arrived and chests of treasure were carried away. A small village of free men nearby produced food to support the operation.

We were led into the mines and shown how to work. It did not take great skill, but it broke a man's body and soul. The tunnels were so deep and extensive that it would take hours to shepherd us down into our work sites each day, so we lived inside the mountain. Throughout the mines various caverns had been excavated, and we often ate and slept in those. Day and night had no meaning—there were only feeding and resting periods. Most of the time a horn was blown to call us from whatever shaft we were excavating back to one of these caverns, where we were given food and a few hours rest. Over time, though, tunnels would collapse and various work crews would be cut off from one or more caverns. When this happened food would be brought to us where we worked, and we would be allowed brief periods of rest after a meal before picking up our tools again.

At first I tried to keep track of how long I had been there, but I gave up after a while. Time had no meaning, nor the cycle of day and night, nor months and years. There was no world beyond the flicker of the oil lamps, the dust and the work. I tried to get to know my fellow slaves, but we were moved around as the work required, and no one knew anything about the world outside the mine anyway. Whoever we had been before didn't matter.

CHAPTER 20

Over the years—for I did realize that years were passing, though I could not say how many—I moved deeper and lower into the mountain. We dug new shafts, ever sloping downward, always in search of the next vein of gold or gemstones. I had no sense of the outer world around me, but from the guards' comments, I gathered that the mines were becoming less profitable, as we extracted most of the wealth hidden within. They were becoming short of labor as well. Many around me died from sickness, accident, or simply losing the will to continue, and the guards told the survivors that we weren't being replaced with fresh slaves.

Eventually, I was working alone. My companions had passed away or been assigned to other sections of the mine. For a long time (again, it seemed like years but I didn't really know) I had been working in an area of the mountain, which contained diamonds. I hadn't found any in a long time; however, I continued to dig for it because it was all that I knew how to do.

It also seemed that the period between feedings got longer, but maybe that was only because of my loneliness. I do know that while at one time there were dozens of guards who would bring us food and carry away the diamonds we found, the number of guards I saw lessened. Eventually, there was only one man that I ever saw. As I said, the gap between feedings got bigger, and I had rarely found any diamonds to show him, anyway. For years I had been blessed with better health and strength than my companions, but as my guard brought me less and less food I grew weaker and lonelier.

At one point (I cannot say one day, for I had no days), I discovered a large cluster of kimberlite–the kind of rock that contains diamonds. It was the largest that I had ever found. I was excited to show it to my guard, for he was the only human contact left to me and I craved human contact. The uncut gems were useless to me, but I looked forward to his excitement and perhaps some extra food as a reward. I rested, looking at the raw diamonds embedded in the rock wall in front of me, waiting for the man to come with my meal so I could point them out. I waited for what seemed like forever. I fell asleep for a bit, woke hungry, and fell asleep again. This went on longer than I could stand. I would sleep, stare at the diamonds in the wall, feel my hunger and thirst and drift off again. I do not know whether this lasted hours, days or weeks.

In one of these spells, I began to cry. I thought of my life before: my father who was so much better to me than I deserved. I never appreciated his wisdom, love or generosity. I was an ungrateful son, and a disappointment to his legacy. I bawled like a child.

I thought of others who had been kind or loyal to me, when I was not kind or loyal to them. I thought of my father's friends and advisors, like Admiral Constante who died defending our family's home. I thought of all the gardeners and guards, cooks and teachers who had doted on me, made my world so comfortable and secure. Gratitude for the life they had provided, and the devotion they had shown, for the first time in my life filled my heart. As if my mind's eye was a bird rising above my own, I saw Monte Saggezza spread out before me. The town and villages, ports and farms full of citizens who made the nation what it was. How their ingenuity and effort produced the nation's wealth, and how they gave a portion of that in taxes to support my lifestyle. Indeed, how all the Saggezzan kings had been blessed by such a productive land and generous people. For generations they had supported our plans and endured our failures. They had given us such privileged lives, for we did not invent, make or grow anything. They honored us as symbols of the nation, and all they asked was that we honor and protect them.

I thought, even, of you Feroxans. How you had shown us friendship for hundreds of years, protecting our northern border so that we could be secure enough to send our ships around the world.

I could see before me in that flickering darkness a great crowd. I saw family members, friends, servants, and citizens. I saw my ancestors, allies, instructors, and lovers. I saw everyone who had given me a strong body and a fine education. I saw everyone who had trusted me, loved me, served me, fought for me, and tolerated me. I saw everyone who had given me plenty of money, great skills, good meals, pleasant times, useful knowledge, and multiple languages.

Ever since I began counting sunsets among the barrels on that ship, I had felt sorry for myself. For years my mind had dwelt on the images of all that I had lost. While I was forgotten in that endless, timeless darkness, I held onto my hurt, my sense of being cheated, and the supposed unfairness of my life.

But at what I figured were my last moments, dying of hunger and thirst alone in the deepest pit of that mountain as the oil in my lamp ran out, I did not feel sorry at all. Instead, I chose to be grateful. I was grateful for what everyone had done for me in Monte Saggezza, and grateful that I was still alive. I don't know why Jalous didn't simply kill me when he took the throne. I had lost so much, but not everything. I even felt something I never considered possible: I felt grateful for the fellow slaves I had known, for friendship and companionship in that place. I even felt grateful for the guards, for small moments of kindness some had shown through the years. It must have been a miserable assignment for them, as well.

As the kimberlite danced in front of me from the flicker of the lanterns' light, it was as if a thousand eyes were staring at me from out of the darkness. My heart was bursting with gratitude for everything that everyone had done for me.

And what had I given in return? For the first time I saw my life through their eyes. I took them for granted. I had abused their gifts and trust for my own purposes. I had lied to them. It had never occurred to me what they needed from me, for I only ever thought about what I wanted from them. As grateful as I felt to them at that moment, would any of them feel grateful for me? I couldn't think of any reason that they should.

I looked down from the eyes glittering in front of me, judging me, and I thought of my hands. They were gnarled, calloused and white as a newborn under the black dust I wore like a second skin. I thought of all the things my hands had learned to do: wield a sword, play music, write documents. Despite the hard work they had done in these mines, they were good hands, and I was grateful for them, as well. One thing that they had never done, I realized, was serve others.

I looked up at the eyes of all those to whom I was grateful. I knew that my hunger was making me delusional, but I vowed to them, then and there, to use these hands to serve. To serve those faces in the dark, all those who deserved better from me. If God would ever let me leave this mine, I swore to him, I would use whatever skill and strength was still within me to serve Monte Saggezza as it had served me. I cried out loud, "Oh God, how could you have given me so much and I responded with so little?"

I was nearly mad with hunger and thirst, but I suddenly realized that what I thought were eyes were actually the array of raw diamonds embedded in the wall of the tunnel, glittering in the lamplight. Years of miner's reflexes took over. With a rush of energy I pulled myself to my feet, lifted my pick and began to swing. As I worked the strangest thought I have ever had came into my mind. I have known delusions and more than once in the darkness took the madness of my own thoughts as inspiration. I tell you that God sent me these words as I removed those stones, "You are the wealthiest man in the world."

My dad was a good man. He worked hard and provided the basics. Like I said before, the conversation was always a little lacking. Growing up was the usual "don't do this, do that" kind of parenting.

There was one habit that I thought was somewhat unusual for him and a little out of his character. With the chip on his shoulder he didn't have much good to say about many others. But he always had me write thank you cards to anybody who had helped me or gave anything to me. Of course there were the birthday thank you notes, and Christmas present thank you notes. I'll never forget on my wedding day; I knew he was proud, there was no question there. I was once again, hoping for a little advice. His advise; "Remember to get your thank you cards out on time." I couldn't believe it.

I guess it made a little sense, hearing the story, knowing that it was imposed on him like a bad religion.

CHAPTER 21

I don't know how long I spent cutting into that cluster of kimberlite from the wall. When I was finished I was more exhausted and hungry than before, and I felt so thirsty I was ready to lie down and die. But my mind was clear, as was my vow. As long as I had strength and skill in these hands, I would serve the people of Monte Saggezza.

As I looked down at the enormous pile of raw diamonds in my hands, I heard God's voice still ringing in my ears. I wasn't sure what it meant, but I was certain that I was the wealthiest man in the world.

I also knew that if I waited any longer for my guard to come I would die of starvation in the dark when my lamp ran out. I badly needed to find food and water. I left my tools where they were, but put the diamonds in a basket we used to collect what we had discovered. I took the lamp, flickering on its last drops of oil, and headed up the shaft, looking for a guard or even another slave.

As many years as I had spent in those mines, I had no real sense of direction in them. It was an anthill of little shafts and tunnels running every which way. We always had the guards to lead us about, and most of us had stopped paying attention shortly after arriving. After a while the only things we cared about were food and rest.

I headed toward an open cavern I did know, where up until recently we had met the guards to be fed, hand over what we had found, and exchange dull tools for sharp ones. That had stopped a while back, with my single solitary guard coming down to where I worked. Now I backtracked to that place, but found no one there. Nor was there food, but I did find water in a barrel. After drinking I realized that as hungry as I was, I was perilously close to dying from thirst. I also found more oil for my lamp.

I sat and considered what to do. Clearly, no one had been here for a while. The only reasonable course of action was to go in search of food and someone who knew what was going on. I didn't fear the guards, since the raw diamonds in my basket were the largest I had ever seen in the mines. Any guards I met would be glad to see me when I handed them over. I was sure they would give me some food and encourage me to lead them back to where I found the stones.

There were markings painted or scratched on the walls at every intersection of two shafts, and the guards used those marks to find their way in and out. But the marks were coded so that the prisoners couldn't use them to find a way to escape. I knew that my survival depended on my breaking that code; otherwise, I might wander in that maze until I dropped dead.

I won't bore you with the details, but I was able to figure out what the coded marks meant. I had always done well with math and puzzles, and this wasn't especially difficult. It was just enough to confuse the slaves, but not enough to confuse the guards. It took me some time and I had to backtrack from some mistakes. Eventually, though, I was able to work my way from one depot and tool room to another, finally making my way up to the main trunk shaft for the whole mine system.

I was confused and concerned because not only did I not see anyone, I saw no sign that anyone had been in the mine recently at all. I wondered if I really could be the last person in the mountain. What had happened to everyone?

I reached the last intersection before the entrance, with an odd, pale light illuminating the floor at the corner. For many years I had seen nothing but braziers, torches, and lamps. I wept at the unforgettable glow of moonlight. I crawled around the bend, expecting to be confronted by armed soldiers but there was no one. I stumbled to the entrance, shading my eyes from moonlight and starlight that seemed impossibly bright to me. I looked down and saw a road leading up from the fortress below, the valley empty and beautiful. Rocks and trees cast sharp, dark shadows and the sky glittered more than any gold or gems I had seen beneath the earth. Below me I could hear the river and I felt a breeze on my face for the first time since I had arrived. I fell down and cried. I fully expected to be pierced at any moment by an arrow from a soldier who had clearly wandered away from his post. If I had died right then, I would have died happy. "I am the wealthiest man in the world," I kept repeating to myself.

I wasn't shot, nor did I hear any shouts. I stared at the fortress and saw no light through the windows or on the walls. It looked abandoned.

This story has grown too long, so let me skip ahead. I explored the fortress and indeed found it empty. I was able to clean myself there and change out of my rags into some spare clothing I found. I walked two miles down the valley to the farming village that had supplied the fort. I found someone who spoke a language I knew, and discovered that there was some sort of civil war going on in that country. The mines, which had stopped being profitable years before, were abandoned and the garrison left in a hurry to fight the rebels in some other province. The villagers had seen the soldiers take a handful of wasted looking slaves with them. I surmised that in their haste I had been forgotten, or considered too much of a bother to fetch, and left to die on my own.

I also discovered that I had been in the mines for eleven years. I had no idea.

The villagers had no love for the rulers of that land, being descendants of a different race, and took pity on me. I stayed with them several weeks, putting on weight, regaining my strength and learning their language. They are another group of people in my life that was kind and generous to me. As I got stronger, I gladly earned my keep and served them by helping with various farm chores.

When I felt strong enough to travel, I thanked them for their kindness, and gave them several raw diamonds from the lot I had brought out of the mountain. They would be able to trade them in the nearest market town for things to benefit the village.

I walked a day and a half to the nearest market town, where I exchanged another diamond for a horse and further supplies. I have always learned languages quickly, and between what I knew of their tongue, plus finding folks who spoke other tongues I knew, I was able to travel northward through that country for many months. I began to learn a few simple trades, and with those skills was able to stop from time to time and take on work in various villages and towns.

And so, for the last year and a half, I have been slowly working my way home. I've spent time in several countries. I have learned much about people and the world that I never would have known living in Castello di San Michele. Many times along the way I have stopped to earn a living and enjoy being alive and free. I am the wealthiest man in the world. But my vow to return to Monte Saggezza has always been in my mind. A few weeks ago I booked passage on a grain ship headed to this port.

I have not come to cause you any trouble, and it's only an accident that I came to stay in your inn. How could I have known that it was *your* inn? It was highly recommended, and its reputation is well-deserved.

You want to know why have returned. I have no clear idea of what I will do. But I know that I owe the people of this country a great debt of gratitude. I promised myself that I would use whatever strength and skill I have to serve them. I pray that I will never become involved in politics again. For the last week, I've been speaking to land agents, searching for a piece of property. I have learned several trades and have in mind to become a craftsman or even a farmer. I want to contribute to a local church. Perhaps I will build a home for widows and orphans, who were harmed by the disastrous things I did to this country.

I hope that no one else recognizes me. I'm surprised that you did. I had hoped that enough time had gone by and my appearance had changed enough. Maybe that's naïve. I'm not afraid to face justice, but I suspect that if Jalous discovers me he'll run me through quickly rather than exile me a second time. I'm not afraid to die; the mines cured me of that. Still, I have a purpose here. Like you, I expect, I'd like to fulfill it anonymously and quietly.

CHAPTER 22

Aquila, Jakob, and Ragnar were silent throughout Diamante's story. When it was clear that he was finished, the whole room was quiet.

"Well," asked Diamante with a slight smile, "am I a threat to you?"

"Maybe," answered Ragnar quickly. "If the government discovers you're here, or the Regnians, it won't just be your life in danger. They will assume that we are conspiring with you in some sort of a coup, harboring a dangerous fugitive. It's worse now that we know who you are."

"I can respect his desire to start a new life," began Aquila, but Ragnar cut her off.

"Then he should start it somewhere else. This is exactly why we can't return to Ferox. In fact, to make it worse, if they discover who he is it will be assumed that the two former royal houses are plotting some sort of a rebellion. He must leave immediately."

Aquila agreed. "Ragnar is right. Whatever your intentions, even if it was an accident that you showed up here, it is close to being a tragic accident, probably even a fatal one. You must go–tonight–and stay away from us. If anyone recognizes you here at The North Wind, we're all in peril."

Diamante nodded. "I understand. It was an honest mistake that our paths crossed," said Diamante. "I have found an agent who represents some property in a valley that is a three-day ride from here. It is a remote region, one that I never visited as king. The likelihood of anyone recognizing me there is small. I'll be leaving in the morning with him to evaluate it. I will not return, and I'll forget that I saw you." He began to stand.

As Ragnar and Aquila stood to say their goodbyes, Jakob remained sitting, cleared his throat and said, "Jalous doesn't have the sword."

Everyone turned. "What did you say?" asked Aquila.

"You heard me. Jalous never found it."

"So what?" said Ragnar. "It's none of our business. We are done with Ferox, heirlooms, and politics. We certainly don't have anything to do with Saggezzan politics. Nor do we want to."

Jakob spoke so quietly it was almost a whisper. "I don't think you can say we are completely done with heirlooms."

Aquila shot him a dangerous glance. "That's enough, Jakob," she snapped.

Diamante hadn't taken his eyes off of Jakob. "How do you know that Jalous never found the Sword?"

"It's a secret, but not a well-kept one. He's never produced it. When he made his first and only trip to Ferox he took an armed escort, and some of them talked. So have Feroxan traders that have come down to the lowlands. He didn't have it with him. Since then, it's never been seen, even on state occasions. He can't produce it. The only reason that anyone—parliament, the guilds, the military, the nobles—accepts him as monarch is that he is backed by Regnian troops."

Ragnar cut in. "But he is king, and Saggezza and Regnian soldiers will drag anyone to prison, or worse, who doesn't recognize that."

Jakob pressed. "He has power, but not legitimacy. This country is dying. I remember Monte Saggezza under King Bonum. I was a young man and it was foreign to me, but it was a magnificent country. Noble, strong, wealthy. The envy of the world. He began running it into the ground," pointing to Diamante, "but Jalous has run it over a cliff. We've been here twelve years. Tell me this place is noble, or healthy. It certainly isn't either anymore. We're doing okay, but we're on a sinking ship. If things don't change in this country soon, we're going to have to think about moving our operations overseas."

Aquila was irritated. "What's your point?"

Jakob grinned mischievously. "I'm not sure that I have a point. I do have a question, though, for you." Once again he pointed at Diamante. "Where's the Sword of Ferox?"

Diamante looked at him for a long time. "I don't know. It was hidden the night Jalous kidnapped me and captured San Michele."

"Yes, you said that," growled Jakob. "Who hid it?"

"Admiral Constante."

"But you said that Constante died in your arms. Did he hide it himself, or did he give it to someone else to hide?"

Diamante shook his head. "Before he died, Constante told me that he had given it to someone trustworthy to hide."

"Did he tell you who?"

"Yes. My father and Constante were all boyhood friends with this man. They grew up together. He was one of the most faithful and loyal men I ever knew."

"Well," reasoned Jakob. "If such a man was given the sword to hide, it seems that he carried out his assignment well."

"What good is this to us?" asked Ragnar, frustrated to have to be the voice of reason.

"Do I have to spell it out?" asked Jakob. "This country is dying under an unjust, usurping king who has sold it to the King of Regno. Jalous has been robbing it, slowly and painfully to death, before our eyes these last twelve years. Against all odds, the legitimate king of Monte Saggezza walks into our tavern, having sworn an oath to repay his gratitude to the people of this country. If that were not enough, he tells us that the symbol of his legitimacy was hidden by one of King Bonum's childhood friends." He waved a finger at Diamante. "Another faithful and loyal servant who served you better than you served him. Someone else you—and all of us—should be grateful to."

"Grateful?" asked Aquila. "Why grateful?"

"Because this man needs to find that sword and serve this country by freeing it from Jalous and the Regnians. They have always lacked legitimacy. This man has it, or can get it."

"I have no desire to be king. That's not why I came back," said Diamante.

"Yes, I know. I heard you. But you've missed the point of your own story. It's not about what you want; it's what you owe this country. Let's not mince words: you were a terrible king, a disgrace and an embarrassment to your father's legacy.

"I know. I admitted that," said Diamante.

"You started this country sliding down a slope that it has never recovered from. Jalous and Regno wouldn't have been able to seize the throne if you hadn't made it so easy by your irresponsibility. You come back now saying that you want to serve the people who served you. To show your gratitude by giving to a people that gave you so much. Wonderful. Prove it."

Diamante just stared. Aquila shook her head, "How is he supposed to do that?"

"Well," roared Jakob, "he's not going to do it by farming and taking in orphans. If he really wants to show his gratitude and serve his country, he can find that sword, get rid of the Regnians and give this country back to its citizens!"

Aquila stared at Jakob for a long time. Then she sat down slowly. Ragnar followed. Diamante hesitated, still halfway to the door. Then he, too, turned and found his seat.

CHAPTER 23

They talked until dawn, before they heard the dining room below come to life. After a sleepless night, Ragnar suggested they go down for breakfast.

The discussion was passionate, even argumentative at times. Diamante wanted absolutely nothing to do with politics, much less trying to challenge Jalous for the crown. His goal really was to live in some remote village under a new name, treating his neighbors kindly and generously.

The three Feroxans pointed out how naïve this was. They admired his honesty, but it was likely that someone would eventually recognize him, just as they had. Word would eventually reach Jalous and the Regnians, and while Diamante may not care what happened to him, those around him would suffer as well. Whatever good he accomplished in some village would be more than undone by their retribution. Endangering more innocent people was no way to show his gratitude for their hospitality.

"As much as you may want to be an ordinary citizen of Monte Saggezza, you aren't and never can be," Aquila pointed out just before dawn, "just as I cannot return and become an ordinary Feroxan again. We were both born royal heirs. We may not want to be special, but we are. If you want to be a craftsman or a farmer, you'll have to do it in some other country, like we have. In Saggezza you will never be anything but King Bonum's heir, the rightful king, and a mortal threat to Jalous and Regno."

"I was a foolish and selfish king," pleaded Diamante, "Saggezzans miss my father, not me."

"But you are the rightful king," Jakob responded. "Your choices are to become a good king, like your father, or pass the crown to someone who would be. Jalous didn't just steal the throne, he sold it to Regno in exchange for being allowed to sit on it as a puppet. Saggezzans deserve to get their country back, with a legitimate king who will guard their freedom and traditions."

Aquila nodded. "There is no one else who can give that to them."

Still, Diamante resisted until they had heard the first delivery carts making their way through the still dark street below. He was finally convinced by considering what gratitude he owed Constante and Master Verde. He had told them about Constante's dying words, and about Verde, who had taken the Sword to hide. All these years, Diamante had assumed that Verde had been captured along with everyone else that night, and that Jalous had found the Sword. He had no idea that it was still missing. Jakob and Aquila argued that his father's best and oldest friends, Constante and Verde, had given and risked their lives to preserve the Sword and keep it from Jalous. They didn't do this for Diamante personally, but for Monte Saggezza. They did it so that Diamante, or some other legitimate heir, could be restored to the throne. "If you are grateful for and have vowed to serve those who have served you," argued Aquila, "then how can you not honor Constante's and Verde's courage and sacrifice? What would they want you to do? What would your father want you to do?"

Diamante had no response, and reluctantly agreed to at least investigate what had happened to Master Verde. They couldn't find the Sword without finding him, or whatever clues he had left behind. What he would do after that depended on the outcome of that search.

Now the four of them sat over a hearty breakfast with steaming mugs of tea, in a nook off of the dining room, strategizing in low voices. There wasn't much to plan: Diamante would go to Avigliana and quietly ask around about what had happened to Master Verde during Jalous' coup. He could not be too direct, or too visible. He would travel on small roads through rural villages, avoiding the major towns he had visited as king where someone might recognize him.

Ragnar volunteered to go alone, since he could travel freely and ask around for Master Verde without raising any suspicions. If he found Verde, he could send for Diamante. But Diamante wouldn't hear of it. He hadn't spent thirteen years in exile only to endanger another friend. Plus, Ragnar was a foreigner with a heavy accent. He wasn't out of the ordinary in a busy seaport, but in the foothills around Avigliana his questions about a servant of the former regime would raise suspicions. Assuming that he could stay in disguise, Diamante could pass for a middle-aged Saggezzan with some innocent purpose. If Verde was alive he might have disguised his identity as well, and if he was dead he might have left behind some clue to the Sword's location. Only Diamante knew the people and places well enough to solve these puzzles.

"I'm going with you," Aquila blurted out. "I'm going with you and will help you with some of my contacts."

"What?" Diamante sounded confused yet encouraged to have her support. "I don't think so. I don't need any distractions." Heads turned to Aquila for her response. "What do you mean, a distraction?" Diamante could feel his face warm and he quickly got up and walked across the room. "I've... I just work better alone."

"Well if you're going to be King then you better get used to working with others."

Diamante knew she was right.

Aquila knew she was going to win.

"So that settles it. I'm going with you."

Everyone at the table was surprised that Aquila insisted on going with Diamante, including her. She insisted that she could help Diamante with various resources, from money to contacts throughout the kingdom. If they had to have any dealings with Regnians or Jalous' officials it was safer for her to do so than Diamante. She had spent the last decade building a reputation and accumulating favors with the government. She had enough business interests throughout the country that she could find a pretense for almost anywhere they needed to go.

What she didn't want to admit to the others was that she was bored. Adventure was in her blood. Starting a new life and making a fortune in business had been enough of a challenge to keep her engaged, but lately the business had become routine. The employees at the inn didn't need her watching over them, and Jakob and Ragnar had their import and export operations well in hand. The idea of going on a quest, especially a dangerous one, excited her like nothing else had in years.

She didn't want to admit to herself that she was attracted to Diamante, or ask herself why she was. All she knew was that she wanted to go with him to find out what had happened to Master Verde.

There was no urgent reason to get started, but no reason to delay, either. They agreed that Aquila should take care of various matters before she left, and give the employees some advance notice. Departing suddenly with a mysterious stranger was exactly the sort of thing likely to attract unwanted attention. To provide cover for their trip, she would send a message to her suppliers in Avigliana that morning, telling them that she would be arriving in a few weeks to discuss business. Diamante would be introduced as a new employee. They would keep a low profile, avoiding the sort of places where someone who had dealt with Diamante as king might recognize them. But they wouldn't sneak around, either. They would, as Jakob called it, hide in plain sight as merchants on busy roads and crowded commercial inns.

They left a week later, riding horses from Aquila's stable, wearing the insignia of her business, and leading a pack animal loaded with sample products. The road was crowded with similar travelers going in both directions and no one paid any attention to them.

Aquila did not tell Diamante about her restless excitement, much less her growing attraction to him. Nor had she mentioned, in all her discussions, that the Sword wasn't the only missing heirloom, and that she had brought the Royal Saggezzan Counting Box with her when she fled Ferox.

CHAPTER 24

They arrived in Avigliana ten days later. Jakob's strategy of hiding in plain sight proved wise, and no one paid any attention to Diamante. Most Saggezzans had never met him face to face, nor had any of the Regnians or other foreigners who had flooded into the country since his exile. With time and the changes in his appearance, he was just another middle-aged merchant.

Both of them wondered how he would feel the first time that he saw Castello di San Michelle overhead. When they first rounded the bend in the road that brought it into view, they stopped and stared. After a bit, Diamante shrugged. "I am the wealthiest man in the world," he said. "Not was, am." He spurred his horse into a trot and Aquila followed.

Like him, Avigliana had changed since his last birthday party. It was still the capitol, but of a diminished and occupied country. The neatly laid out streets still lay along the lake, and the red tiled roofs still stood out against the white backdrop of the mountains. But the energy of the marketplaces was lower, and there were no impromptu speakers or political debates raging in the tree-lined squares. Artists and parliamentarians no longer lingered in street-side cafés. The whole city felt more business-like than busy. Regnians were everywhere, looking arrogant but bored. Sullen, frustrated Saggezzans did what they must to get through the day without any enthusiasm for their work.

On the way, Aquila and Diamante had come up with a better way to inquire about Master Verde than knocking on doors and gossiping in taverns. She would conduct her business as normal. She would keep meeting with suppliers to negotiate prices, and with Regnian officials about licenses and taxes. In the course of her dealings she would casually mention that she was building a villa on the coast, and needed someone to design the grounds and gardens. She would say that various people had recommended a former royal gardener whose work was legendary, and ask if anyone knew where she might find him or one of his trained apprentices. They would follow whatever leads that produced.

Diamante acted as her employee, taking care of the horses, handling the samples, and taking care of the arrangements at the inns and cafes. There was danger that in Avigliana someone might recognize him, but Aquila had an idea.

That night she called him into her room. It wasn't unexpected. Each night they would talk of their plans for the next day and would often spend a couple hours reminiscing about their earlier years.

"I'm concerned about someone recognizing you here." she said with her back towards him.

"I agree." Diamante said. Aquila turned. Diamante was now looking into her eyes, noticing her tenderness. "What do you think we should do?"

"I have some hair dye; I think it's the least we can do." She motioned for him to come near. She had already gathered a bucket of water that was heated by the fire. Diamante sat in a chair and let his head slowly fall back into her hands.

"Is it too hot?"

"No, it's perfect." He relaxed as she ran her fingers through his thick brown hair, turning it a charcoal black.

Both of them became a little lost in a moment they had both somewhat hoped for.

After she dyed his hair, he quickly got up, thanked her, and went to his room. Neither one mentioned the evening the next day. They both went on their way and continued their search for the sword.

Aquila's inquiries didn't seem to make anyone suspicious. The gardens around the castle had been dismantled almost twenty years earlier by Diamante, but if anything, their reputation had grown legendary. It was not unreasonable for a wealthy foreigner to want someone who could lend prestige to her new villa. Unfortunately, no one knew where Verde was or how to find him. During the chaos of the coup and the Regnian occupation, many officials of the former regime had died, disappeared, or been exiled. Aquila did not dare press the issue or seem too eager. Instead, she sighed with the irritation of the rich woman who can't find good help, and asked if Verde had left behind any trained apprentices who "could design in his classic style."

That produced one lead. A banker she was having tea with recalled another client who wouldn't stop talking about a wonderful estate they had visited which reminded them of the old royal gardens. Aquila reacted perfectly, gasping with the thrill of a wealthy collector hearing that an obscure but valuable piece of art might be available. The banker gave her the name of his other client, and the three of them met the next day for lunch on a private terrace over the lake. A few hours later she had the name of the estate, which was a three days' ride from the capitol. Using the same cover story, Aquila sent a message to the estate by courier the next morning. The following day they set out at a leisurely pace to avoid attention.

Their message had arrived ahead of them, and the owner of the estate, a Regnian official, was only too happy to show off his gardens to a wealthy merchant of Aquila's reputation. They took Diamante's breath away. They weren't a copy or miniaturized version of the royal gardens by any means. But the same care, attention to detail, and genius of design were all evident. The words that came to his mind were "the same love created both these places." No, he thought, "The same love created both these places."

In his role as Aquila's assistant, it wasn't his place to speak. She, of course, had never seen the Saggezza gardens and had no idea of what he was thinking. She praised the gardens effusively, and fed the owner's pride effectively. He invited her to stay for dinner. Diamante, as a servant, could of course join them as well. His role simply required him to stay quiet and attend Aquila. But while the banquet was being prepared, they found a few minutes to talk privately on the terrace. Diamante assured her that those gardens were the work of Master Verde. They were on the right track.

It was a long evening, listening to the Regnian official brag, denigrate Monte Saggezza, and patronize Aquila. She half expected him to try to extort some sort of bribe from her in order to stay in business, as so many of the Regnians did. But she mentioned the names of enough her contacts above him in the government that he must have thought better of it. For her and Diamante it was painful, because they wanted to ask about who had created the gardens and their host showed no inclination to discuss it.

It wasn't until dessert that the subject came up. After another round of praise for his genius at having created such gardens, she asked the official who he had hired to "carry out the work." He clearly did not consider such "tradesmen" (as he called them) worthy of his remembering their names. But he did tell her that his steward had hired them from another town upon recommendation.

"There was more than one, then?" asked Aquila, with idle curiosity.

"Yes, I believe there was. A few brothers, three perhaps, and an elderly father. A family business of sorts, I suppose."

"I would be most grateful if you could help me to find them. I want them to reproduce, if they can, what you created here. Giving proper credit where it's due, of course," smiled Aquila.

The flattered Regnian sent for his steward, who appeared and remained standing while his master interrogated him on Aquila's behalf. He only remembered the first name of one of the sons, the one who handled business for the family. The family had been recommended to him by a Saggezzan land owner while he was overseeing construction of the estate. The family had come from a nearby province, hired local laborers to assist them, and completed the work during the late spring and early summer. They had stayed in tents on the grounds so as to work longer days. When the project was complete he had paid them in gold coins, and they had moved on.

The next day, Diamante and Aquila left carrying a note of introduction to the estate in the next county which had recommended the gardening family. Again, they found a garden that could only have come from the heart and mind of Master Verde, apparently being assisted now by his sons. That owner did not know how to find them either, but supplied another lead. Diamante and Aquila continued their search.

CHAPTER 25

Every lead gave them another piece of the puzzle. Master Verde had survived the coup, and began working with his sons. They traveled about, earning commissions to design grounds and gardens for estates, government buildings, abbeys, and even public parks. They had no real fixed residence, and found work by word of mouth and personal recommendations. It sounded as if he had three sons who were apprentices, or had even taken over leadership of the business. One in particular handled the interaction with the clients. They had several wagons of tools and supplies, camped in large tents on the job sites, and worked like ants from dawn to dusk before moving on to the next project. They hired local laborers for the hard work. None of the clients had ever spoken directly to their father. He was visible each day, either giving directions from either a large table in the camp, full of plans and drawings, or walking around the project, teaching and directing the workers.

They talked to some of the laborers who had been hired, and they knew nothing of the family's whereabouts, but they all described working with the father in the same terms. He was gentle and soft spoken, but firm and unyielding in his insistence that things be done perfectly.

He genuinely seemed to love the land, and to love what it was being shaped into. He was a teacher, a task-master and a visionary. Everyone who worked for him, though, said that they felt as if he had served them more than they had served him. He had a way of looking inside each of them and knowing how to bring out the best, even if that was sometimes a painful process. Every man said that working for the traveling gardeners was the best job they had ever had.

At every project they visited, Diamante saw Master Verde's hand more clearly. Diamante remembered growing up in the gardens at San Michele, playing, hiding, and getting into mischief. As he got older, familiarity bred contempt. But after his decade spent underground in the mines, tears came to his eyes each time he walked through one of the landscaped creations. The inspiration behind each design was to not unnecessarily change the land or create an artificial environment, but to draw out the natural characteristics, to enhance them so that the visitor experienced the best of the property's essence. He thought of how he once heard a sculptor describe his work as releasing the statue hidden in the block of stone. That is what Verde's gardens were like.

After more than a month of searching, the most recent lead Diamante and Aquila could find was almost two years old, and the trail was going cold. It was fall, and the work season was almost over. Perhaps the Verde family worked in the south during the winters? Perhaps they had a home somewhere and spent the winters resting? Diamante and Aquila needed a fresh lead.

They finally got a lead three days later talking to a stonemason. He had recently been commissioned to do stone work in a garden at a new estate to be built the following spring. He had requested written plans of the gardens so that he and his apprentices could begin precutting stones over the winter, and had been directed to get them from a man in a small town in a southern valley. The name of the man was the same as the son who handled the clients for the Verde family. Diamante leaned forward in the tavern where they sat with the stonemason, and asked how recent those instructions were.

"Two days ago. They told me to contact this man to get drawings and dimensions of the garden plan. I was going to send one of my sons there next week to get them."

Aquila and Diamante thanked the mason and bought him another round just before leaving. Even though it was only late afternoon, they decided to check out of the inn and ride to the next village before dark. Aquila suggested they press on into the evening and reach the village beyond that.

They rose at sunrise, saddled up and continued. Riding aggressively, they reached their destination on the fourth day.

They took rooms at an inn and asked the innkeeper if he knew the man. The name wasn't familiar, but when they described the family of gardeners, traveling in tents, he knew who they were talking about.

"Oh, them. I figured they were just a bunch of tinkers. Staying out on the abbey grounds, they are. Abusing the hospitality of the Abbot, I think. Bad enough with all of these foreigners taking over the country. We don't need batches of tinkers camping around the countryside, scaring the milk cows, and stealing, and what not."

The horses were saddled again before the groom had finished rubbing them down. *The innkeeper was probably still ranting about tinkers,* Diamante thought as he and Aquila trotted briskly up the hill to the abbey.

Beneath the abbey, on a level spot before the vineyards began sloping down toward the river, were a half dozen tents and wagons organized into a circle. As they approached, they could smell a cook fire and hear someone sharpening tools on a grindstone. But what struck them most were all the children. There were dozens of children playing, laughing, talking, and running. The children didn't all appear to be related, either. They were of various colors and ethnic backgrounds, and some seemed to be chattering in foreign languages. This wasn't a typical sight on an abbey's grounds. They wondered if the Abbot had begun taking in orphans.

They reached a low hedge around the entrance to the abbey, which seemed to be designed to keep some goats near the building to keep the grass down. Two monks were hoeing a vegetable garden on the front of the property. They looked up, greeted Diamante and Aquila, and asked if they could be of assistance. By their clothing, the monks could tell that they were well-to-do merchants, and asked if they had an appointment with the Abbot.

Diamante thanked them, but said they were looking for Master Verde. One of the monks smiled, and gestured toward the tents and wagons. Diamante thanked the monk, and asked pleasantly if the abbey was operating an orphanage. The brother smiled but shook his head. "Oh, goodness no! The children belong to the gardeners. The Abbot lets them stay with us whenever the gardeners visit to work on the grounds." He smiled. "It brings life to the old abbey, doesn't it?"

Diamante and Aquila dismounted and tied their horses to a post near the hedge. They stood watching for a moment at the children playing. There were also some adults working and cooking in the center of the camp. A few of the kids were kicking a ball back and forth, and one boy booted it high over his companions' heads. It landed in the middle of the circled tents, where some women seemed to be laying out a meal on long tables set on saw horses. A moment later, a small, old man emerged, carrying the ball. He was thin and wiry, with his skin dark and creased by the weather, but he was spry and walked with an easy energy. The children saw him, shouted, and called for their ball. He looked for a moment like he would toss it, but with a twinkle in his eye he drop kicked it, soaring it high above them. The kids squealed with delight and ran about, looking up, jostling each other to be the one to catch it. Four or five boys fell in a tumble, laughing, as the ball landing on top of them. The old man threw his head back and laughed so loud the monks hoeing the garden looked up, and laughed as well.

Without saying anything to Aquila, Diamante walked slowly toward the man, who was still watching the children. As he approached, the old man turned.

The two of them stood looking at each other. The man's smile faded quickly, and Diamante's expression was inscrutable. They regarded one another for what seemed to Aquila a very long time. Then Diamante lowered his head. She couldn't tell from where she stood if he was bowing, or weeping, or both. The old man responded by sinking to one knee and bowing his head.

Some of the children looked, wondering what was going on, as did the monks. A few of the women also looked up from where they were setting the table.

It was as if time stood still. Then, Diamante dropped to both knees like a sack of grain thrown to the ground, reached out and fell into the embrace of the old man. They stayed that way while everyone watched and wondered.

Diamante spoke, "Master Verde, my Lord."

Master Verde interrupted, "Yes, my King."

"No, Master Verde, I am no king."

"You are your father's son. Therefore you are my king."

"No Master Verde, please stop. I am not here to be a king. I am here for one reason only."

Diamante paused as his heart raced.

"Yes, my king?" asked Master Verde with the tenderness of an old friend.

"Please stop, please, please. Please forgive me." And with that he wept. The broken Diamante tucked his face in his knees as his tears wet the ground.

Master Verde held Diamante as he sobbed.

"My king, I forgave you the day you retired me. Why would I ever walk with that stone in my shoe? You are forgiven. You always have been."

My father had walked with a limp for most of his life. He told me it had something to do with a blister that he never took care of. Somehow it got infected and of course being as stubborn as he was, he never went to the doctor to have it looked at. After a while the limp affected his back and he never walked the same. It's hard to walk a straight line with a crooked back.

I wondered if he felt the metaphor being lived out in his life. I wondered if I was walking with a stone in my shoe.

CHAPTER 26

Aquila played with the children in the pasture below the Abbey as the sun set. She hadn't kicked a ball since she was a child in Ferox, where they played a similar game. She found herself laughing as the kids ganged up to pass around her and score goal after goal.

Over dinner in their wagon camp, she had learned that these children–almost two dozen of them–were Master Verde's grandchildren as well as many orphans the Verdes had adopted. This Abbey was a sort of permanent camp, where his daughters-in-law and the children stayed while Verde and his sons were away on construction projects. The Abbot provided hospitality and the Verde family worked on the Abbey's properties and made generous contributions to its charities. Many of the adopted children were foreigners of various races that the Abbot found on his trips to the port cities. Since it was against the Abbey's rule to take the children in, the Verde family did so gladly. The monks ran an informal school for the children, all of whom were literate and moving on to advanced studies. They were also learning valuable trades in the abbey's various operations.

Now, as Aquila was losing a football match and having the most fun she had enjoyed in years, Diamante was walking with Master Verde and his three sons in the vineyards. During supper, Master Verde had not allowed discussion about Diamante or Aquila. He had introduced them as special guests and old friends of the family and left it at that. After a prayer of thanksgiving, the feast was served on long tables set up between the tents. A number of the brothers from the Abbey had joined them; it was a noisy affair with forty voices competing to tell jokes and stories. After the meal, a few of the children brought out instruments and played a piece of music that they had been working on with one of the monks. Then everyone helped clear the tables and those whose turn it was to wash and clean did so while the others went into the pasture with Aquila to play before it got dark.

As the family dispersed, Master Verde motioned for his sons and Diamante to follow him, and they walked through the rows of vines.

The Abbey's vineyards were vast, and as they strolled up and down the hills, Diamante told his story, much as he had to the Feroxans that night in The North Wind. Master Verde and his sons listened, interjecting questions here and there to clarify certain points. Master Verde seemed intensely interested on more than one level. He wanted to understand as much as possible about the details of what had happened, where it had occurred and who had been involved. Beyond that he was keenly paying attention to not only what Diamante had to say, but how he said it. As they walked he turned his head to watch the former king's body language, and stopped to look him in the eye as he answered some of the gardener's questions.

He was quite curious about Aquila, as well. During their search, she and Diamante had talked about whether they should reveal her identity to Master Verde when they found him. They had concluded that since they needed

Master Verde to trust them in order to reveal the location of the Sword, they would have to in turn trust him. Diamante had her permission to share what he knew. His questions made Diamante think that Master Verde suspected there was something Aquila was holding back, but he never asked her directly about the Saggezzan Counting Box.

The three of them returned to the camp several hours later. The children were in bed, and so they sat in the tent that served as an office for Master Verde and his sons. A table was full of plans and drawings, and more were rolled up and stacked with books along the walls. They drank tea and continued their discussion far into the night until Master Verde finally told everyone it was time for bed.

After breakfast the next morning, Master Verde and his sons headed off to work. They were helping the monks dig a well and construct an innovative tile-irrigation system for a new section of vines and fruit trees terraced on a high slope, more than a mile above the Abbey. He invited Diamante to join them. The Abbot offered Aquila a tour of the Abbey and its properties. She spent the day fascinated at the diverse and complex operations: a scriptorium where manuscripts were copied, working farms producing all sorts of fruits, nuts and vegetables for markets, shops that made textiles and metalwork, a hospital for the poor, orchards and vineyards producing jams and wine, beehives for honey and wax, and several parish churches that served the local villages.

Diamante spent his morning at the bottom of the hole digging the well, and his afternoon laying baked clay tiles into irrigation trenches. After more than a decade in the mines Diamante was skilled and surprisingly cheerful doing this type of work. Master Verde never raised the subject of his identity or the Sword.

They lived this way with the Verde clan at the Abbey for several days. No one discussed the reason for their visit. Diamante labored beside the Verde family and the monks and Aquila spent time with the Abbot and his managers. She even made agreements to market the Abbey's products in the ports and abroad. Meals were in the open air, and everyone had time for reading, conversation, and play in the evening. Diamante sat outside by the fire at the end of each evening, going through his ritual with his counting box. When Aquila asked him how he was doing, he grinned and replied, "Haven't I told you? I'm the wealthiest man in the world."

Indeed, it seemed to Aquila that they all were. While the Verde clan didn't have the type of surroundings or privileges that Diamante or Aquila were used to, their lives were clearly wealthy and wonderful.

After supper on the fourth evening, Master Verde asked Diamante and Aquila to follow him into the abbey. They met the Abbot in his private office. After they were all seated with cups of honeyed tea, Master Verde spoke.

"Father Thomas is trustworthy, and I have confided our dilemma to him. He recognized you anyway, sire. You may not remember him, but he was a young friar who assisted in the chapel at Castello di San Michele the year after your father died. He is a dear, old friend."

Diamante nodded, waiting for Master Verde to continue.

"Let me answer your question directly, and then we may speak of other things."

Diamante looked at Aquila with questioning eyes knowing he had yet to mention the sword of Ferox.

"I did hide the Sword."

Diamante's shoulders slouched as he exhaled. Master Verde had seen what was not spoken.

"Jalous' men never suspected that I had anything to do with it because you had retired me from service quite some time before the night of the coup. They searched for years, but it has never been found, and after this long I suppose that they have given up looking." He paused, sipped his tea and everyone waited for him to continue.

"But I know where it is."

The Abbot's study was very quiet, and everyone found something different to look at: Aquila at the Abbot, the Abbot at Master Verde, Master Verde watched Diamante and Diamante stared absently out the window at the monks taking honey from the Abbey's beehives in the meadow below.

"After much thought and prayer, I have decided that I will not tell you where it is, nor lead you to it."

CHAPTER 27

Aquila's heart skipped a beat, and she stifled a gasp. Father Thomas's expression was unreadable, and his eyes were fixed on Master Verde. Diamante smiled faintly and shrugged slightly.

"I was convinced I had to find you and seek your forgiveness. I wondered about the Sword," Diamante said slowly. "I'm not sure that I really wanted to find it. That's not why I returned to Monte Saggezza. Now I can move on and discover what's next in my life. Thank you."

"That's what I'd like to talk about," said Master Verde. "What will you do now?"

"As I told you the other night, I hope to find a way to serve my country and the people who gave me so much; to be useful. To produce more than I take from this world."

"That's a worthy ambition," replied the old gardener. "Do you have a plan?"

"Like I said, I've considered buying a piece of property in a remote village, and taking up farming or a trade. I've learned many new skills."

Master Verde looked him directly in the eye. "I'd like you to become my apprentice."

Diamante had no reply. He breathed deeply and held it in as if to hold back a painful reaction. Aquila looked back and forth between them, confused.

"Join my family and me. Work with my sons. This abbey is a safe place, and no harm will come to you under Father Thomas's protection. Your life will be productive, and you will serve me, the abbey, and our clients. It will be honest, hard work. You will be a free man with a simple life. No one will know who you are. You will have a place with people who will love you, and in time, I hope that you will love them."

"As for you, young lady," he turned to Aquila with a twinkle in his eye, "you are more than welcome to join us. My wife says you and he make a nice couple, and Father Thomas is able to perform weddings, though I don't think he gets much practice." Master Verde laughed and the Abbot laughed out loud.

Aquila blushed and stammered. "I... I've been gone from my business too long. My partners need me. And Father Thomas and I have agreed to partner together on some ventures."

Master Verde gave a look of exaggerated disappointment. "My wife will be devastated. I think that you'll be back, though, and not just to meet with Father Thomas."

He turned to Diamante. "Well, how much time will you need to consider my offer? I'm in no hurry, but your first reaction is almost always the most honest."

"I accept," Diamante said, looking him in the eye with a grin. "Nothing would make me happier. As I tell her," he nodded toward Aquila, "all the time, I'm the wealthiest man in the world. And once again my wealth has increased."

"Well," said Aquila, not wanting to admit that she felt hurt, disappointed, and confused, "I suppose that I'd best turn in, as I probably should leave first thing tomorrow." She began to stand.

"Please wait." Master Verde held up his hand and motioned her to sit back down. "I'm not finished." Father Thomas leaned forward over his desk, chin in hand, looking at Master Verde with a curious expression.

"I didn't say that I would never take you to the Sword. Just not now."

"When, then?" blurted Aquila, confused, frustrated and embarrassed by this whole journey and her feelings for Diamante.

"When it's the right thing to do. Maybe soon, maybe never. I don't know."

"I don't understand," said Diamante, shaking his head. "I'm happy to be your apprentice with no expectation of ever getting the Sword."

"I know, and that's why I offered you the job. But it very well could be that the best thing you can do for yourself and everyone else is to retrieve it and use it to heal this country. But I'm not convinced that you're ready. You can't bring health to this nation until you are healthy. You've come a long way, but I don't think that you're healthy enough yet. When will you be? I honestly don't know. Maybe never. But I will watch you, work with you, live with you. If the time comes when I believe you have the character to restore your father's kingdom, I'll take you to the Sword."

Diamante looked concerned. "I don't want to be your apprentice only for the hope of becoming king again. That wouldn't be honest. I would be only using you and the Abbot. I've used too many people."

"Leave that to me," said Master Verde. "Forget about the Sword. We will never talk about it again, unless I bring it up. Assume that you will never see it, that you will never return to the throne. Be the best apprentice gardener you can and have no goal beyond that. Work, love, pray, and rejoice."

Master Verde clapped his hands and stood. The meeting was over.

The next morning Aquila and two of the monks, with a wagon load of sample products from the abbey, departed for the coast. There were hugs and kisses with Master Verde, his wife, and the rest of their family. Father Thomas blessed her and she promised him that his monks would return in a few weeks with orders and contracts. She and Diamante did not know how to say farewell, and the moment was strained and brief. She promised to return soon for a visit, but she couldn't say when. She almost blurted out that she had changed her mind, that she would sell the business to Jakob and Ragnar and stay with him. But neither of them could take the step of sharing their growing feelings with the other. In the end, a quick peck on the cheek and a forced cheer was all they could manage.

Diamante settled into his new life as an apprentice to Master Verde and his sons. He worked on landscaping projects with them around the Abbey during the day, and he also shared the other trades he had learned. The monks taught him some new skills and he became a competent craftsman in a number of fields. He shared his love of sports with the children and taught them some new languages as well. The following spring, he went with Master Verde and his sons to work on a series of landscaping projects around the country. Diamante didn't interact with the clients, instead working with Master Verde in their field office or beside the laborers. He had never been happier in all his life.

Aquila returned to The North Wind and immersed herself in her businesses. The high quality samples from the abbey were well received by the traders she worked with, and she sent the monks back with enough orders to fund the abbey's charities for a year. She missed Diamante desperately but admitted it to no one.

As Monte Saggezza's economy floundered and its people became ever less free and more dispirited, Aquila's businesses turned record profits. She may have been the richest woman in the country, but she never felt like the wealthiest person in the world because she wasn't with the man who was.

CHAPTER 28

One day, as summer gave way to fall, the old gardener told Diamante that it was time to right a great wrong.

More than a year had gone by without Master Verde speaking to Diamante about anything concerning his former life as king. They spoke openly and honestly but only about their present lives. They talked about their work, Master Verde's family (which they both came to consider Diamante a part of) and the Abbey, which was their home when they weren't traveling. Diamante shared his growing fondness for Aquila, whom he wrote to often and managed to see every few months. Sometimes Diamante shared things he had seen and learned during his years of exile. But he had no interest in talking about Castello di San Michele, the Sword of Ferox or the monarchy, and Master Verde never brought them up in the many questions he continuously asked Diamante.

One day in late summer they returned to the Abbey for a few weeks between projects. The monks prepared a banquet under the tents. There were happy reunions between husbands and wives, and between fathers and children. After supper the blacksmiths from the Abbey looked over the landscapers' tools and made plans to repair them, and Diamante and Master Verde's sons made lists of improvements that the monks needed done around the Abbey and its grounds.

Master Verde pulled Diamante aside, and suggested that they take a walk through the vineyards. After they had walked a bit, Master Verde began.

"You have grown into a fine man. Your father would be proud."

"Thank you. I wish that I could have seen him through the eyes I have now. I would have understood him more." He fell silent.

Master Verde continued. "You are enough of a man that you can, and should, try to fix some of the things that you left broken. It's not possible for you to undo the past, or repair every harm. But there is something that you can do. It will be painful, and risky. But it would be good."

Diamante wondered what the gardener was leading up to. He felt a heaviness, because he had broken so many relationships. He wondered if this was about the Sword. He hoped it wasn't. But all Diamante said was, "Of course. What can I do?"

As they walked, Master Verde told a story that astonished Diamante.

When Diamante had been a reckless young king, he had had love affairs with many young women. One of those had been Admiral Constante's daughter. Constante, whose duties shuttled him between the palace and the fleet, had not suspected. Diamante had betrayed his father's best friend and the kingdom's most faithful official. The young woman had loved Diamante. Diamante, living in his illusions, often lied to her by promising that someday he would marry her while he continued having affairs with other women. During the last, disastrous year of his reign, she had discovered that she was pregnant with his child. She pleaded with him to save her from shame but Diamante refused to marry her. She was devastated, of course, but she was also too frightened of the wild, young king and her powerful father to reveal the affair. Diamante quietly gave her some money and sent her away to a small village at the far end of the country. She refused to tell Constante who the father was, and the admiral had died before the baby was born. Afterward, it had been too dangerous to reveal to the boy, or to anyone else, that he was the bastard son of the exiled king and grandson of the dead admiral. It would have made the boy a target for Jalous and the Regnians. Now the mother and son lived anonymously, in near poverty, in a forgotten country town. She worked as a housemaid and the boy was a reckless youth, running in the streets with a gang of friends.

Diamante was shocked at what he didn't know and what Master Verde did. He remembered the girl, of course, and sending her away a few weeks before the coup. He hadn't known what had happened since. His heart was painfully conflicted.

Master Verde told Diamante that he had known about the affair with Constante's daughter all along from the network of palace servants, among whom it was no secret. After the exile, and from time to time since then, he had inquired about the welfare of the mother and boy. After several months of Diamante working for him, the gardener had become convinced that the former king had become teachable. Now Master Verde wanted him to become truthful. It was time to tell the truth to the boy.

Diamante accepted that the boy and his mother should know the truth and that he should provide for them. "But I fear for them. What if she or the boy talk to others, and reveal that I have returned and the boy is my son? If Jalous and the Regnians come for me, then so be it. Ever since I returned, I have accepted that that day might come. But Jalous would love to eliminate Constante's daughter and my son; to eliminate a potential threat, to make an example, for pure spite. I cannot bear to think that these people, who have already suffered enough because of me, might suffer more."

Master Verde was ready for this objection. He responded that if Diamante ever did regain the throne, it was better for the boy to meet and know his father first as a man, not as a king. If Diamante never became king again, then the boy deserved to know the truth and meet his father. It would be a difficult conversation for everyone involved. He must introduce himself to Constante's daughter and her son, making whatever amends and letting them know him as an ordinary citizen, but they would need to keep that knowledge to themselves, at least for the time being. Everyone concerned would need to be honest yet discreet, and because Diamante had caused this brokenness, he had to take the first step in fixing it.

"We will be here at the Abbey for at least two weeks. You must go and do what you can to heal this wound. You won't be able to heal it completely, but you can begin."

The next morning Diamante saddled his horse and set out. It was a two-day ride, and he spent it grieving for all the people he had hurt. He had no idea how to heal the wounds in Constante's daughter and his son. He didn't know what he would do or say when he found them, or how they would receive him. He couldn't imagine that they would be happy to have him show up on their doorstep.

Helping them financially was the easy part: he had made good wages with the Verde family and spent little, and he had a fortune in diamonds left from the mines, hidden with Father Thomas at the Abbey. Constante's daughter and his son would be well-provided for, and he would see that the boy received the best education available. Yet he knew that while money might ease their lives, it could never really heal the wounds of shame and abandonment. Because of his parents and the circumstances of his birth, he would struggle to belong anywhere.

And what did he owe to Constante's daughter? He remembered the girl, of course. Her name was Tessa. The truth was, however, that he didn't remember very much about her beyond that. There had been many girls, and Diamante had used them without ever really knowing them. What was the right thing for Diamante to do now? Marry her? Someone he had barely known, fourteen years earlier? But to make her an unwed mother with a mysterious source of income would be to subject her to further gossip and ridicule.

And what about Aquila? He had grown to love her, but was afraid to admit it to anyone for fear of causing her trouble. In Monte Saggezza he was a stranger, hiding in the shadows, who could not afford to have anyone look too closely at him or ask too many questions about his background.

As Diamante rode, he realized that while he may have changed as a person, he was still a problem to everyone around him, especially those he cared for.

CHAPTER 29

The second evening after leaving the Abbey, Diamante arrived in the town where Tessa and his son lived. He checked into an inn, had a quiet dinner and spent the evening by the fire, still examining his feelings and his options. Before heading up to bed he took out his counting box and spent some time using it, as he had done every night since leaving the mines.

The next morning he rose and went to the market in the main square. Master Verde had given him the name that Tessa and the boy were living under, and Diamante wanted to make some inquiries about them. As always, he couldn't attract too much attention to himself for fear that someone might recognize him. Diamante didn't know what sort of background Tessa had invented to disguise her identity, and he didn't want to say anything that would contradict her story. He had given a lot of thought to what he could say that wouldn't arouse anyone's suspicions.

He bought some gifts in a few market stalls and casually mentioned to the shopkeepers that his father had worked with Tessa's father many years earlier (which was true enough). Since Diamante was going to be traveling through the province, his father had asked him to look up his old friend's daughter and her child to see how they were faring, and bring a few gifts on his behalf. He asked the merchants for advice in picking out the gifts since, Diamante said, he had never met either of them personally.

That got a few of the shopkeepers gossiping, and what he learned broke his heart. Apparently Tessa (they knew her by her assumed name) worked on and off as a domestic servant. She had trouble keeping a job for very long because she was known to be a sharp and bitter woman who drank too much. She fell in and out of employment, sometimes housekeeping with a wealthy household but more often cleaning inns and taverns. She seemed depressed, and after drinking she could become belligerent and irresponsible. When she had arrived in the town, fourteen years earlier, she had purchased a home, but it was run down and badly needed a new roof. The boy, named Mario, was emerging as the leader of a group of local boys involved in mischief and minor crimes. At thirteen, he was tall, handsome, and charismatic. He was also a trouble-maker and petty thief. He hadn't committed any major offenses yet, but the town sheriff was already becoming familiar with Mario. His mother was unable to control him and, without a father, Mario seemed destined for a life of no good.

Diamante knew this was his fault. When he had learned she was pregnant, he had arranged for a friend to buy her a small house far away and give her a bag of gold, if she would swear to never tell anyone who the father was. She was afraid enough to comply. Constante had raged and tried to discover the secret, but only a few weeks later he was killed, defending the Kingdom and the Sword of Ferox. He had died in Diamante's arms that night, and as he did, Diamante had said nothing about how he had betrayed King Bonum's best and most loyal friend. Now, all these years later, Diamante was tasting the bitter fruit of his youth. Tessa and Mario lived on a diet of lies and rejection.

There was no right time or way to have this conversation, so Diamante decided he might as well do it as soon as possible. He had learned that Tessa was currently working nights in a tavern, cleaning up after it had closed, and was home during the day. He went to her house early that afternoon. It was probably an attractive little place at one time, on a lane in a working class neighborhood. But it had become dilapidated with neglect and the neighbors probably considered it an eyesore.

He stood at the door. The packages of food and gifts felt weak against the backdrop of her needs. He took a deep breath, knocked and waited. No response. He knocked again, and after a while heard someone shuffling about. The door opened and he saw Tessa.

She had been beautiful once, he remembered. She had been the daughter of the country's highest military official and the young king's secret mistress. Before she came here she was one of Monte Saggezza's elite and had never wanted for anything. She was still a well-built woman: tall with a noblewoman's bone structure. Now she was broken and dispirited. She slouched, and when she glanced up years of heavy drinking were traced on her face. He had obviously woken her, and she was not happy about it. "Well?" she asked after he said nothing for several seconds.

Diamante had rehearsed this conversation in his mind, trying to find a way to gradually ease into the topic. Now he couldn't remember any of that.

"Here." He handed the food and gifts to her.

"What's this?" she responded with annoyance, "We don't need your chari—" Diamante interrupted her.

"Tessa?"

She jerked as if she had been slapped. She had not heard that name for fourteen years. She wasn't that woman anymore. He watched shock, then fear, then recognition play across her face.

"Is it you?" she whispered, staring confusedly at him.

For the next two hours they sat in her kitchen, drinking weak tea. Diamante confessed and apologized for everything. He told her how he had hid the story of their affair from her father, the coup, how the admiral had died defending the throne and the Sword, and how he had kept the truth from his father's friend even in his last minutes. He didn't feel that he had a right to ask her for forgiveness. It was for her to decide if and when she wanted to give it. He told her of his exile, his journey back to Monte Saggezza, and his new life. He told her how he had found her.

It was late afternoon and the sun was low enough to come directly through the dirty windows. Tessa moved her chair to keep it out of her eyes. The conversation stalled.

"Well, what happens now?" Tessa asked wearily. She badly wanted a drink.

Diamante was adamant that he would provide for them. Money was not a problem, but their safety and well-being was. With Diamante back in Saggezza, there was a greater risk that their identities could be exposed. If Mario learned the truth, could he be trusted to keep the secret? If the word leaked out, how long would it take before Jalous and the Regnians would have him and Tessa arrested, or worse?

From her description of the boy, Diamante already recognized too much of himself in Mario. He worried about what kind of man Mario would become without a father's influence and good role models. Even with those advantages in his life, Diamante had not turned out well. Without them, Mario's future looked bleak.

"What have you told Mario about his father?"

Tessa had always told her son that his grandfather had been in the navy, which of course was true, and was lost at sea, which was not. His father, she had maintained, was a sailor who had died at sea, in a shipwreck.

Diamante had begun to form a plan, but he realized that he didn't have the right to decide her fate again as he had so many years ago. He wanted to help, to fix her and Mario's life, but he knew that while he could offer help, he couldn't make them accept it.

"What do you want, Tessa? I can give you money, but you and Mario need more than that. I tossed you into this place, this life, like rubbish. In the name of both of our fathers, I can redeem you out of it. In the name of my Father in Heaven, I will–if you'll let me."

She said nothing for a very long time, staring out the window into the shadows deepening in the lane. After a while she raised her head and looked him in the eye. He saw something of her father's determination rise to the surface.

"This place. There is nothing to keep me here. I stopped hoping for myself a long time ago. If you can give Mario a better life, we will go wherever you say."

Diamante sat back in his chair, thinking for a few minutes. When he leaned forward he shared his plan. He wanted to introduce himself. He wanted to tell Mario that he was his father and accept the boy's hurt and anger. Eventually he hoped to earn his trust. The last thing he wanted to do was to tell him one more lie, but the boy was immature. As long as he was in this town he might say something to his friends in the streets. For his own safety Diamante had to tell him one more lie, at least for a couple of days.

CHAPTER 30

When Mario came home that evening, he stopped in the doorway and stared suspiciously at the tall stranger sitting in the kitchen with his mother. Diamante could see that Mario was trying to figure out what sort of trouble he was in.

Tessa introduced Diamante as someone who had known her father, and Mario's father. From there, Diamante picked up the tale that he and Tessa had agreed to, full of half-truths. As his mother had told him, her father, his grandfather, was in the navy. What she hadn't told him was that he was a ship's captain. Diamante had served under him, and the captain had saved his life once, rescuing him from desperate circumstances. Since then, Diamante had spent many years traveling in foreign lands. Now he had returned, and come into good fortune, with a nice estate by the coast, just a week's ride away. He wanted to repay his debt to the captain's family by offering Tessa a good job and a decent home there, and an education for Mario.

Mario was confused and angry. Diamante could see the questions in his eyes: *Who is this stranger? Is mother seriously considering this? What about my friends?* When he spoke, though, his first question cut Diamante to the heart.

"You knew my father?"

"Yes," Diamante answered. "I knew him. He was... lost...on a journey far to the south, just before you were born." Neither of them said any more.

Mario and his mother argued for nearly an hour. She told him that this was the best opportunity she would ever get to give him a decent life. Diamante tried to help her in front of Mario without appearing to be a meddling stranger. He answered questions about who he was and where he was taking them as vaguely as possible. Eventually Mario stormed out, slamming the door. They heard him running down the lane, calling to his friends. Diamante's instinct was to run after the boy, but he knew that he couldn't. Tessa left for work and Diamante returned to the inn, praying that his plan would work out.

It took two more days of arguing and cajoling, but eventually Tessa convinced Mario to come along willingly. They had few possessions worth taking along, and Diamante left the keys of the house with the priest of the local church with instructions to sell it and donate the proceeds to the poor. He bought a small wagon to hitch to his horse. Four days after he arrived, he left town with Tessa and Mario, taking a road for the coast.

They continued that way for a few hours until they reached a crossroads, well beyond anyone who might recognize Tessa and Mario. He stopped the wagon and turned to Mario.

"My estate isn't on the coast. But my home is only two and a half days by this wagon to the north and west, against the foothills."

Mario eyed him suspiciously. "Why did you lie to me?"

"Your mother and I agreed that it was best to keep our destination secret until we left the town, and anyone you might tell. It's important that I keep the source of my fortune a secret." Diamante paused. "I became wealthy on a journey far to the south, and..."

"In the place where my father was lost?"

"Yes. I found my money on the same journey—in the same place, in fact—where your father was lost."

"Were you there when he died?"

Diamante hesitated. "I was." He paused. "It's important that I keep the story of this wealth secret."

"Were you and my father pirates?"

Diamante laughed. "No. We were many things, but about the only thing that we weren't was pirates. I was telling the truth about providing your mother a good job, in any trade of her choice, and a decent home for both of you. And whether you like it or not, your mother and I have agreed that you will get a first-rate education. I know this is hard for you to understand, but please be patient. I'll tell you more when we get there."

Mario looked at his mother, who smiled and nodded. He didn't look happy, but seemed caught up in the adventure of it all as Diamante chose the road that headed northwest.

On the morning of the third day, the wagon began passing cultivated fields and the homes of tenant farmers. There were workshops for craftsmen, blacksmiths, and weavers. They saw beekeepers and wineries, and everyone they saw looked free and happy. It was orderly and productive and reminded Tessa of Monte Saggezza when she was a little girl.

They approached a line of hills covered with fruit trees and vineyards, with the Abbey nestled in among them. Diamante stopped the wagon and turned to Tessa and Mario with a smile.

"The fields and villages you've seen for the last hour belong to the Abbey. It leases the land to those people, who are free tenants. The Abbey runs a cooperative to market their products."

"This is my estate. Well, actually it isn't mine, but I do live here and have a rather unique relationship with the Abbot."

"You said that you would give us a house, and my mother a job," Mario said warily.

"I will. There are dozens of trades practiced on the Abbey's lands. I will purchase a home for the two of you and set her up in whichever trade or business interests her. The Abbey runs a first rate school, and you will attend it.

"But," said Diamante as he flipped the reins and the wagon moved forward again, "first you must meet my friends. Well, they're more like family. And then we need to see Father Thomas, the Abbot. We have a lot to talk about, and we're going to need his help."

Over the next few days, Tessa and Mario got to know the Verde family and the monks, and Diamante had several long talks with Master Verde and Father Thomas. The Abbot was confident that they could help both the mother and the boy. Time, trust, and the hard work of listening healed many hurts: the Abbey had been restoring people for centuries. They would be safe and well-cared for. As he promised, Diamante made financial arrangements, leasing a home for Tessa on the Abbey's land and providing everything she needed to begin whatever sort of trade or business interested her. He was not abandoning her again; he would continue to live on the Abbey grounds with the Verde family and be involved in her and Mario's life.

It was time for Mario to know the truth. His curiosity about his father couldn't be put off any longer. A few days after Tessa and Mario were settled in, the three of them sat down with Father Thomas in his study. Diamante confessed to Mario that he was his father, and told him the entire story of how they had all come to be there that day. It was a lot for a thirteen-year-old boy to absorb, but Tessa and Father Thomas were there to help.

It was both a painful and hopeful season. Tessa, Mario and Diamante's lives changed dramatically. It wasn't easy, and there were setbacks, but all of them moved forward. With Father Thomas's help, Tessa stopped drinking and became an accomplished potter. Mario struggled to shed the bad habits he had learned in the streets, but the Abbey's school kept him too busy for mischief and he grew into a successful student. Diamante visited him every day, regularly providing words of affirmation reminding his son of the man he was to become, and over time Mario came to trust his father as they became very close.

Diamante had to initiate another difficult conversation, with Aquila. He told her about Tessa and Mario. Mario would always be his son, but Tessa was a friend whom he had a responsibility to support. He was falling in love with Aquila, and hoped that it wouldn't impede their growing romance.

My dad got up again. This time I got up with him. It was like both of us didn't want to address our level of transparency, or the lack thereof. I wasn't about to admit to him that we were going bankrupt, and he wasn't about to admit that his dad was right.

Keeping your cards close was a family tradition. "Not airing your dirty laundry" was something that I had learned to live by. Unfortunately, it always seemed to catch up with my dad, and now it was catching up with me.

CHAPTER 31

Diamante had worked for Master Verde for almost two years when the old man asked him one day to accompany him on a trip. Diamante asked where they would be going, but the gardener refused to say.

"Do you trust me?"

"Of course."

"Then just come with me, and hold your questions. Plan to be gone for a week."

Diamante packed and told Mario that he would see him in a week. The next morning, Master Verde and Diamante saddled a couple of the rugged mountain horses that the Verde family owned and followed a back road leading higher up into the foothills.

Their route took them to the lower ranges of the Feroxan Mountains, where they turned to the east, following the range toward the capitol city of Avigliana. For two days Master Verde led them along an old hunting trail that Diamante remembered from his youth. Around their campfire each evening Master Verde asked questions like he usually did. Diamante did his best to answer each of of Master Verde's questions, covering the past two years of life lessons. The master gardener was more the master questioner, drawing out the truth and wisdom from each story and situation.

The third morning, the trail ascended steeply out of the hardwood forests on the lower slopes and across ridges covered with pines and boulder fields. Above them the buttresses of the Feroxan Range were covered with spring snow and seemed close enough to touch. Diamante had fond memories of hunting for bear and mountain goats as a teenager with his father in this very area. He remembered that over the next few hours the trail would go above the timberline, switchback to the top of a granite-strewn ridge, and soon Castello di San Michele and Avigliana would be visible, just a day's ride below. He wondered what Master Verde had in mind, but held his questions, as promised.

Just before noon, they crested the ridge. The chilled wind whipped at them on an exposed rock far above the timberline. They paused nonetheless to admire the view. The bottom of a glacier hung not a thousand feet above them, obscuring the jagged peaks from their vantage point. The view below and ahead of them was spectacular. The trail cut switchbacks across a steep slope of loose rock, disappearing in a forest of tall pines. Below that there were a series of ridges, stepping downward, each one a bit lower and covered with more dense foliage. Four or five ridges below—Diamante remembered that it was exactly a six hour ride from this point—they could see San Michele standing like an island. Below that, in a valley dotted with little lakes, lie the red-tiled roofs of the capitol city.

Diamante looked at Master Verde and raised an eyebrow. The older man just nodded, and started his horse down the trail.

Master Verde stopped on the last ridge above the castle, two thousand feet and a two-hour ride to the bottom.

He told Diamante that they would stay there that night, on the edge of a hardwood forest with newly budded spring leaves. After they set camp, Master Verde walked a few yards away to an overlook on top of a large rock. He pulled out a flagon of wine and they shared a cup. They said nothing for several minutes, staring at the countryside below.

"You've done well, Diamante. Your father would be proud of you. You've become the same kind of man he was."

Diamante nodded and said nothing.

"You're the same kind of man, but you don't hold the office he did. You're not the king of Monte Saggezza."

Master Verde was obviously working toward some point, and Diamante waited for him to get there.

"The Sword of Ferox is close by. Before I show you where, answer one question for me: what will you do if I take you to it?"

Diamante didn't jump at the opportunity. The truth was that he was simply happy with the way things were. He worked hard and loved the people that he lived and worked with. He knew that they loved him, not because of his bloodlines or office, but because of the character and quality of his life. Telling the truth to Tessa, Mario, and Aquila the previous summer had been painful, but his relationship was growing with all of them. He slept better than he ever had. For the first time in his life he was content.

Master Verde saw his hesitation and understood it. "It's because you don't *want* to be king, that you *should* be King. You're ready for the responsibility, not eager for the privileges."

Diamante said nothing for a long time. They refilled their wine cups and watched the shadows of the clouds drift across the valley.

"I need more time to answer the question. It's not something I've thought much about."

Master Verde nodded. They stood and walked back to the camp and began making supper.

The conversation that evening was ordinary, but Diamante was more reserved than normal. That night he spent more time than usual fussing with his counting box before going to sleep, as if he were checking his sums many times over. Over the last two years Master Verde had never asked him about this curious habit, and tonight didn't seem like a time to break Diamante's concentration.

The next morning, when the gardener awoke, Diamante was not on his bedroll. He arrived a short time later, having caught a couple of trout from a pool in the stream about a mile away. He put the fish over the fire and the two had a fine, but quiet, breakfast. Afterward, they took mugs of hot tea, sweetened with honey from the Abbey, and walked back to the overlook.

Diamante began. "I'm ready to answer your question."

As they watched the sun rise, light filling the valleys of Monte Saggezza, Diamante talked slowly and deliberately. He began with his concerns about what would happen if he retrieved the Sword. He had many. What would happen to the people he loved, and who trusted and depended on him? Tessa and Mario would be in danger, as would Father Thomas and the Abbey and all its tenants.

He was in love with Aquila, and hoped to propose to her that summer. Their marriage would have to be kept quiet—perhaps she could live within or near the Abbey—but how might retrieving the Sword affect her partners at The North Wind and their businesses and employees? For that matter, what would happen to the kingdom and its citizens? If it started a war, which was the most likely outcome, should the people of Monte Saggezza have to endure even more conflict and suffering? When the battles came could he fight against Saggezzan citizen soldiers, caught in the difficult position of defending the government against a revolution, even if he was King Bonum's son?

For an hour he talked, evaluating and measuring the potential damage that might come from him retrieving the Sword and revealing his identity. Never once during that time did he express concern for his own safety or well-being.

Diamante stopped and sat looking at the country below, now washed in mid-morning light. Master Verde wondered if the conversation was over. After a few minutes, Diamante began to answer the question that had been put to him the afternoon before. He sketched out a plan that he had worked out during the night and on his early morning fishing trip. Point by point, he addressed all the concerns that he had just raised. He knew that there were risks and things that he didn't know and couldn't predict. He was honest about his plan's shortcomings, but he had thought through contingencies in case he failed to accomplish any of his main objectives. The main feature of the plan was that he himself would take the biggest risks, and he would do whatever possible to protect innocent citizens and the people that he loved.

When Diamante finished it was noon. Master Verde stood and stretched. He suggested that they have a bite of lunch and pack up their camp. Diamante asked where they were going.

"To get your Sword, of course."

CHAPTER 32

Master Verde had said that the Sword was nearby. Diamante didn't know what to expect, really. Since they were in the foothills, he thought that perhaps it was hidden in a cave on some rocky crag, or buried in a chest underneath a boulder or tree. But after they saddled up, Verde began riding downhill, following the trail that led to San Michele.

After about half an hour they came to what had been an apple orchard. It had been abandoned many years ago, and though the orderly rows of trees remained, they were overgrown and surrounded by tall weeds and wild brush. Diamante recognized it as the outer edges of what had been the old royal gardens. When he became king after his father King Bonum died, he had pulled the laborers out of the orchards and put them to work building his fairgrounds. After having spent the last two years as Master Verde's apprentice, his gardener's eye was offended by the neglect of the old orchard. As he rode through, he thought of ways to make it beautiful and productive again.

They rode quietly, running straight as an arrow, and crossed a stream with a tiled bed and brickwork along its banks. It was part of an aqueduct system that brought the cold snowmelt down from the foothills and supplied constant pressure to the system of ponds, channels and fountains throughout the gardens. It was choked with weeds that made little dams and reduced the flow. They crossed over it on a little stone bridge, carved with whimsical figures of birds and squirrels. They passed through a brickwork arch in an overgrown hedge and entered another precinct of what had been the world-famous Gardens of Monte Saggezza.

Both men were quiet. The gardener looked about with fond memories, saddened by what had become of his life's work. He could not help picking out what was wrong and what needed to be repaired. Diamante, on the other hand, looked horrified. Having grown up with the gardens, he had never appreciated the value of them and he had failed to honor this gift that been handed down through the royal family. Now he had become quite a gardener himself, with calluses on his hands and dirt under his fingernails. He was appalled at how this masterpiece had been taken for granted and then abandoned.

They rode over a grassy embankment, dotted with benches and gazebos that had given a view over one of the hedge mazes. Coming down the other side, they dismounted and walked along a winding canal that people used to paddle along in little boats, hanging paper lanterns on them after dark on warm, summer nights. But now the water was foul, and ugly shops had been built along the canal to sell alcohol and trinkets to visitors waiting to get into the amphitheater that sat where the hedge maze had been. It had all fallen into ruin. Storms had blown shingles from the roofs, loose shutters hung at odd angles, and youths—who had once come here for the rowdy concerts and parties that Diamante had promoted in the amphitheater—had carved vulgar words and pictures into the paint. Now the paint was fading and peeling. The buildings had been built quickly and with little craftsmanship. Now it all looked cheap and shabby.

"Why did I do this?" Diamante asked himself aloud. Neither he nor Master Verde answered the question.

They slowly rode through the rotting and abandoned fairgrounds, eventually arriving at the central lake. It was perfectly circular, a quarter mile in diameter with a marble promenade that had been lined with shrubs elaborately trimmed into the shapes of animals. In the center was a circular island of almost two acres, with an elaborate fountain whose structure was more than sixty feet high. Diamante had built more ugly shops and alehouses along the promenade and had held wild parties on floating pleasure rafts in the waist-deep waters. Now, the dirty water was full of old garbage and a wet crust of green scum while insects buzzed over and bred in it.

Master Verde reined to a stop on the cracked promenade. He turned to Diamante.

"Wade out to the island. Along the base of the fountain, facing due North, there is a statue of a bear rearing onto its hind legs. Slide the bear backwards."

Diamante did as he was told. The mud sucked at his boots, and he almost lost them more than once. When he sloshed onto the island, he was covered up to his knees with moss and scum. The stench of the water nearly made him gag. There were dozens of animal statues arranged around the base of the immense sculpture. He found the bear, facing due north, and leaned against it. Like all the statues on this level of the structure it was carved of black marble, gilded with gold and about three feet tall. The soles of Diamante's boots were now too slippery to give him any traction. After changing his position and grip several times he finally got it to budge. After a few more tries he had moved it a foot, flush against a wall behind it. On the top of the pedestal where it had been was a loose tile. He looked back across the promenade to Master Verde, who was standing as still as a statue himself with the horses. Diamante used his knife to pry it off. He reached into the pedestal and felt an oiled leather bag. He pulled it out and laid it on the top of the pedestal. Again using his knife, he cut through the laces which ran the length of the bag and which had become too brittle to untie.

Inside he found a huge, heavy broadsword. It was a brutal-looking thing with a dull, charcoal-colored blade. On the thick hilt were ancient rune signs, insignias of battles from fierce, northern lands. The Sword of Ferox.

Diamante slid the bear back into place and wrapped the sword back into the leather container. He waded across the pond to where Master Verde stood, watching quietly. Neither of them spoke as Diamante hid the sword in the rest of his baggage. They mounted and rode back the way they came, to the aqueduct channel they had crossed on the edge of the old orchard. Diamante reigned up, and Master Verde stopped beside him.

"Master Verde, I won't even try to put my feelings into words. It would be too difficult and would be too sentimental. We will meet again soon, at the Abbey. Look for me in three weeks, and tell Mario that I'm sorry I had to stay away a bit longer than I anticipated."

Diamante looked along the stream, running gently downhill toward the lower regions of the gardens. "This morning I told you what I would do if the sword came into my possession. It has, and now I must do it. As I said, I'm going straight to La Spezia to warn Aquila. Hopefully she'll listen and go to the Abbey. Jakob and Ragnar will introduce me to trustworthy merchants and guild leaders there. I'm going to reveal myself and the sword and begin building support. If I can rally enough of them, we can take La Spezia and keep the Regnians from resupplying Jalous or bringing reinforcements in from overseas. In any case, I'll come to the Abbey within three weeks with whatever forces I can raise to defend it. Father Thomas, the monks, your family, and the tenant families must not face any reprisals for having sheltered me."

"Blessings. You are your father's son," said Master Verde.

They looked each other in the eye and nodded. Diamante turned and trotted quickly along the stream, while Master Verde headed into the orchard, back the way they had come.

CHAPTER 33

Diamante followed the old service trails along the edge of the gardens in the setting sun. While it would be disastrous should anyone recognize him, he thought it quite unlikely. In the fifteen years since he had been overthrown, age and life itself had greatly changed his appearance. He was dressed in the clothes of a gardener, and there was no reason for any casual observer to take note of him. Still, this close to the castle he couldn't take any chances. Darkness had set in, and taking the shortcuts he learned as a boy, he made his way through the dark down to the main highway leading out of Avigliana and rode until midnight. He stopped at a working-class inn along the side of the road, and that night he spent more time than usual making his calculations with the counting box.

The next morning he wrote a letter to Aquila, and posted it by an express courier ahead of him to La Spezia. He saddled up and fell in among traffic, appearing to be just another middle-aged laborer riding along the road.

He pushed his horse, and two days later traded it in for a faster one in a market town. He picked up the pace and managed to arrive in La Spezia a week after he had parted ways with Master Verde. He headed to The North Wind, eager to be reunited with Aquila and anxious about what would happen next.

Aquila had received his letter two days earlier, and had already made up her mind about some of its contents before Diamante arrived. In it, he had asked her for the names of leaders in the port that could be trusted, but she had already contacted some and arranged a meeting. He had given her a list of supplies for which he needed sources, and she had already begun to gather them in one of her warehouses as well. He had also told her to prepare to move to the safety of the Abbey, but she had no intention of going into hiding. She was prepared for an argument, and she was prepared to win it.

It had been two years since she had met him and they had gone off in search of the sword. Now that he had it, Diamante was unsure how their relationship would be affected. When he arrived in La Spezia, they had supper with Jakob and Ragnar in her office and talked about the meeting that Aquila had arranged for the next night and the supplies that were being gathered. Afterward, Jakob and Ragnar left, and Diamante and Aquila sat alone to talk.

He wanted her to be somewhere far away and safe when the fighting started. She laughed at the idea.

"I am a warrior, from a race of warriors, and my family has led the Feroxans in battle for six generations. If I see the Abbey during this war it will only be to defend it, not to hide in it. We are not going to talk about this. Let's move on to the next topic."

Diamante slumped. "I cannot put you at risk."

"You don't. I put myself at risk. I said move on."

"But... you don't understand. I don't want to be king. I've come to realize that what I want isn't the most important consideration. But there are some things that I do want, and I can't bear the thought that what I am about to begin could be ending those."

"Whatever are you talking about?" Aquila asked with exasperation.

"I love you." His eyes filled with pain and passion, with a look that could only be given after years of wanting and waiting for the one woman he was meant to be with. A look that begged and hoped that she would feel the same way. That she would choose him as he had chosen her.

That night Diamante asked Aquila if she would marry him. With tears in her eyes, she eagerly agreed, but not on the terms he proposed. He wanted her away from La Spezia, safe at the Abbey until the war was over. Then they could be wed, if he was still alive. Aquila countered that they should get married right away, and fight side-by-side to whatever outcome the war brought. They debated for hours, but in the end Aquila prevailed, and they agreed to get married as soon as possible.

The next day, nearly a dozen of the most influential leaders of La Spezia crowded into Aquila's office. Since she did business with these people everyday, she had reasoned that it was better to hold the meeting in plain sight than to skulk around some warehouse at midnight and raise suspicion. There wasn't anything unusual about this gathering except for the number of people invited. Every one of them was hand-picked, however, for their loyalty to the traditions of Monte Saggezza and their willingness to restore the country's ideals. She began by outlining their mutual frustration with Jalous and the Regnian occupation. Then she called for her special guest to come in.

No one recognized Diamante when he first entered the room. As he began to speak, some of their eyes began to light up as they recalled his face, voice and manner. He told them his story and showed them the Sword of Ferox. He asked for their help, and told them that he would lead them, but that they needed to lead as well in order to restore Monte Saggezza. He acknowledged that his life, as well as the future of the country, was in their hands.

Aquila had picked this group carefully. Every one of them pledged secrecy and loyalty, but they needed to know what he was proposing. Diamante laid out his plan. If they tried to reverse the coup by capturing the capitol, the Regnians would send reinforcements through La Spezia and keep Diamante pinned far inland against the mountains. The key was to capture and hold the port. Without it, Jalous could not be reinforced or resupplied. They could begin to recapture the country from here, and pin down Jalous in the castle.

They all agreed to the plan, but argued that it was premature. A small army had to be recruited in secret, equipped, and organized. It would take a month to organize the men and materials to be able to take the port in a decisive blow and then be able to hold it.

Aquila told them about the supplies she was already gathering. It was a good start, but only a start. They need to recruit more conspirators and organize a secret leadership. They should also organize resistance cells in a few other key towns who would know what to do when they took La Spezia.

Diamante was adamant about one thing. He had no hesitation in risking his own life, but the people at the Abbey would suffer reprisals for having aided and sheltered him. He needed to send a force to defend it.

Everyone was given assignments and the meeting broke up. Afterward, Diamante and Aquila made some plans of their own.

A week later, the foundations for the uprising in La Spezia were being laid. Diamante and Aquila left Jakob in charge and rode out early one morning. They rode as long and hard as their horses could bear, stopping in a town several hours after sunset for food and sleep. They had sent word ahead to this inn, and the next morning fresh horses were ready to continue their race to the Abbey.

On the morning of the third day, they met up with Ragnar. They had sent him ahead a week earlier, and as instructed, he had used money that Diamante had given him to hire a band of Feroxan mercenaries. He had only been able to round up fifty of them, but had sent messages and expected three hundred more mounted Feroxans within ten days. Diamante, Aquila, and Ragnar galloped to the edge of the Abbey's lands. Ragnar divided his force to guard the likely approaches, and Diamante and Aquila continued alone to the Abbey itself.

Two days later, the chapel was overflowing with the monks, the Verde family, Mario, Tessa, and Ragnar—as well as many other friends from the Abbey's lands. Father Thomas performed the wedding, and the Verde family hosted the reception on the sawhorse tables in the vineyard. It was a golden day, a joyful day, and past, present, and future troubles were put aside.

Diamante and Aquila spent the following day with Mario and Father Thomas. They talked about the boy's future and the Abbey's defense. The mercenaries could not hold the place indefinitely, but three hundred and fifty mounted Feroxans under Ragnar's command could beat back anything other than a full-scale assault, which

Diamante thought unlikely. Once La Spezia was taken, Jalous couldn't afford to send a large force on what would be nothing more than a mission of spite, to punish the Abbey for having helped Diamante.

The next morning, the newlyweds rose to embrace a life together, whatever wars were waged against them or their beloved country.

CHAPTER 34

"Who is the fool responsible for this?" King Jalous screamed and threw his cup against the wall. He stood there, fuming, and then without warning grabbed the edge of the table and flipped it over, spilling food, drink, plates, and pitchers across the floor and onto two of his senior advisors' laps.

"Is our commander another traitor, or just incompetent? I want him punished. TODAY!" He panted as he crossed the room and slumped into a chair.

He had just been told that the army he had sent to retake La Spezia hadn't even reached the port city. As they approached the pass through the coastal hills, a half day's ride from the city, they had met with numerous ambushes, hit-and-run strikes from the steep hillsides over the road. The column had been forced to reorganize again and again. When they neared the summit of the pass, fifteen hundred feet above and ten miles away from La Spezia, they found it well-defended with newly built fortifications.

This was the second force which Jalous had sent to retake La Spezia. The first force had entered the narrow, twisting streets where they were attacked relentlessly by defenders on the rooftops and in the unfamiliar alleys. They retreated, confused and bloody, harassed by guerilla attacks for three days as they retreated inland.

It had been three weeks since the uprising in La Spezia. It had begun with the ships in the harbor. All the Saggezzan and Regnian naval vessels had been quietly boarded two hours before dawn, when the sailors and marines were on shore leave or drunk in their hammocks. The town woke to find all the fighting ships in the harbor manned by rebels and flying the colors of old King Bonum. With their officers arrested by the rebels, the half-drunk and half-asleep marines were confused with no one to tell them what to do. They were captured in groups of one and two as they made their way stumbling through the streets.

There were two forts that defended the port, but their defenses faced outward, toward the sea. With the town and the ships in the harbor in rebel hands, the soldiers in the forts could do little but lock the street-level doors and hide inside. They surrendered the next day.

With the town taken, Diamante addressed the townspeople in the main square and met with smaller groups of leaders and influential citizens. He told them his story, of why and how he planned to liberate Monte Saggezza from Jalous and the Regnians. He asked for their support. Most of the people rallied to him, with a good number of the Saggezzan soldiers, sailors, and marines as well. Of course the Regnians were belligerent, but many of them were merchants or sailors with families. If they would swear an oath of peace, they would be allowed to stay. If not, they would be put on merchant ships and transported to the nearest neutral port and set free.

Members of the Regnian or Saggezzan militaries who would not join the rebellion were imprisoned for the time being, but with dignity and under humane conditions.

Diamante moved swiftly after that. He sent letters to every province in Monte Saggezza, to the parliament, to the Church, and of course to King Jalous. He listed the outrages and oppressions that had been done to the country by Jalous and his Regnian masters. He outlined his story and claimed that he was still the rightful King, since he had been removed illegitimately and possessed the Sword of Ferox. He pledged to help the Saggezzans to take their country back. Once they had, he promised a constitutional government and promised to subject his leadership to approval by the Parliament.

He moved quickly to capture Monte Saggezza's two other ports. While La Spezia was the largest and best on the country's coast, there were two other lesser harbors that could be used by the Regnians to resupply Jalous. One of them opened its gates and willingly joined Diamante's cause, and the other fell after a two-week siege from land and sea.

Aquila had gathered a substantial force of five thousand experienced soldiers and militia and taken them to the Abbey. She had relieved the Feroxan mercenaries, but many of them agreed to join the cause and follow her and Ragnar. She also established a second base of operations in that province, up against the foothills. The province had always been one of the most traditional in the country and deeply loyal to the memory and values of King Bonum. The citizens there gladly rose up and joined the revolution led by Diamante and his Feroxan wife.

Three months after it began in La Spezia, Jalous and his Regnian allies were cut off from the sea and fighting a two-front war. Without outside reinforcements or resupply, the people of Monte Saggezza alone would decide this war.

Jalous was a very old man who had never been accepted by the people, much less loved. While the people had disliked Diamante, most had developed a disdain for Jalous and the Regnians, who occupied the country. Their independence, traditions, and wealth had all evaporated over the last fifteen years. The revolution appealed to patriots who wanted to see Monte Saggezza return to its traditional values, and to those who had lost so much that they had nothing left to lose. Those who had managed to make a living under Jalous and the Regnians still had something to lose, and were afraid. Those who had profited under the new regime wanted to protect their investment.

At first, the rebellion consisted of guerilla attacks, seizing things like crossroads, mills, and aqueducts. As the war progressed, there were open battles. Diamante led from the front in every engagement, but gave standing orders to destroy as few Saggezzan lives and property as possible. He refrained from the type of brutal tactics that other generals might use to win a decisive victory.

And so, over the next few months, the country remained divided. Diamante held the coastal ports and most of the rural counties that preserved the old ways. But the towns and cities, where the craftsmen and manufacturing guilds were based, refused to join the rebellion. Without the ability to export their products, their income was shattered, but they were still too afraid to risk being on the losing side.

Monte Saggezza was at a stalemate that Christmas. Diamante held about half the country. The cities could not bring themselves to take a risk by trusting him. But they were starving. Without the ports or the farms, economic activity had ground to a halt. Diamante would not starve Saggezzans for the sake of his rebellion, and he arranged for the cities to purchase enough from the countryside to keep everyone fed. Across the nation, Christmas was a frugal and somber holiday that year. Most of the armies on both sides had gone home, and with the winter bringing either snow or rain for much of the country, no one knew when hostilities might start up again.

Diamante and Aquila spent Christmas with Mario and their friends at the Abbey. Tessa was welcomed into their home, and Master Verde's sons, who had gone off to fight with Diamante, were home as well. While there were many things in their lives to be grateful for, Diamante grieved over the conflict and feared that in his desire to save Monte Saggezza he might actually be destroying it.

Was it time to give up? If only more people had joined him. Diamante expressed his disappointment to Master Verde, beginning to make excuses for what had not been accomplished. Master Verde spoke. "Lead like your father, as if the kingdom depended on it. Leaders who can't lead manage. Jalous cannot lead, so he manages. He manages every aspect of the people's lives because he offers no vision. Those who cannot manage make excuses. Stop making excuses, because those who run out of excuses blame others, and once they blame others, they never go back—or should I say, rarely go back—to leading. Now lead.

CHAPTER 35

"This is a terrible idea. I don't trust them."

Jakob leaned forward and pounded the table between them. "Once that gate closes, any Jalous loyalist or Regnian thug can end this war with a single knife stroke, or hold you for ransom. What do you propose that we all do if they threaten to kill you unless we turn La Spezia over to them?"

Diamante and his senior advisors stood around the map table in his headquarters tent. Their army was camped outside the walls of Varano, one of the most important cities in the country. Varano was famous around the world for producing exquisite metalwork and intricate machines. Other than the capitol of Avigliana, Varano was the most prominent city who had refused to recognize Diamante's claim to the throne. The craftsmen, businessmen, and financial community were afraid to trust him, and the city was full of Jalous loyalists, Regnian agents, and a large garrison of Regnian troops.

All winter, heavy wet storms had blown ashore, dropping snow in Monte Saggezza's higher elevations and endless rain in the valleys. The civil war had stalled, and the country was wet, muddy, and hungry. Diamante could not bear to see the people suffer any longer, and had come up with a plan to end the conflict. Jakob spoke for all his advisors who thought the plan was foolish and reckless.

Three weeks prior to this meeting, Diamante had raised as large a force as he could from the provinces that supported his cause. They marched to Varano and surrounded it. Diamante did not wage a typical siege. He allowed food shipments to enter the city, and the sick to leave. Diamante and the army had blockaded Varano this way for more than a week, without attacking or making demands. The defenders stared over the walls, wondering why he wasn't attacking. His own troops wondered the same thing.

Diamante was making a point. After ten days, he sent a messenger to the city gate with a letter addressed to the city council. It said that he had proven that he had the ability to besiege and destroy Varano if he wanted to, and that no forces in the area were going to arrive and rescue them. He had only one demand: that he be allowed to enter the city alone and unarmed, and speak to the citizens in a public assembly. If they would give him a safe and open audience, and allow him to speak freely, he would withdraw his forces from Varano.

He got no response for five days. He imagined that his demand was causing quite an argument in the city. His army intercepted half of a dozen couriers attempting to escape through his lines and the underground tunnels to carry urgent requests for help to Avigliana. Diamante broke the seals, opened the letters, and politely had his own messengers return them to the city gates, with updates on how his forces commanded all the roads, tunnels, and trails leading into the valley in which Varano was situated. The point was clear: no help would be coming.

On the sixth day, the city sent out a delegation consisting of the mayor, the captain of the city garrison, and the chief Regnian agent for the province. Diamante's soldiers disarmed them and escorted them to his headquarters. They announced that the city would meet his demand, and allow him safe passage and opportunity to speak to the citizens in the town square. They wished to negotiate the details, as well as to secure his promise to withdraw his forces afterward. He had them escorted outside so that he could confer with his advisors, and now they waited in the mud in the center of his camp.

Diamante smiled at Jakob. "Of course we can't trust them, but that's the whole point of this war. A country can't function without trust and there can be no trust without risk. The people, leaders, businesses, schools, military—trust is the blood that keeps the body politic working.

"Monte Saggezza used to be a great nation because its heart beat with integrity, as each person trusted the one they lived with and worked next to. Not because everyone was flawless, but because they all believed in something bigger than themselves. The people knew that God watched them and held them accountable for what was seen and unseen. They also knew that the country was the sum total of all their actions. To fail yourself was to fail your fellow citizens.

"I broke that. The people stopped trusting me and the government because I was untrustworthy. That's how Jalous, who is not trustworthy either, was able to seize power. Once I had betrayed my office and nation, the only thing left was money and power, and Jalous took it.

"Don't you see? The only way to heal this country is to restore a sense of integrity, and it's my responsibility to initiate that. I cannot ask anyone in Monte Saggezza to trust me unless I show that I'm deserving of it. And to do that, I have to show them that I am willing to risk my life to earn their trust and serve them.

"This is not a tactic or strategy. The only way that I can ever consider being king again is to show the people that I am here to serve and honor them. The only way I can earn their trust is to risk trusting them first.

"If they capture or kill me, you must take the town by force. This isn't about me; it's about the free people of Monte Saggezza fighting to take their country back. Treason and oath-breaking must be punished. You will carry on. In the end, this is their war, not mine."

At noon the next day, Diamante approached Varano's main gate alone and unarmed. He was met by the mayor, who shook his hand, and a phalanx of soldiers who formed a box around him. There was no conversation. The entourage began moving down the main street toward the city square. The buildings along the street were all four or five stories tall, with the higher floors jutting outward. It was like walking through a canyon that narrowed near the top with almost no sunlight reaching the street level. The soldiers opened a path through crowds eager to see Diamante. People leaned out of windows, stood in doorways, and filled the intersections. There was no cheering, but no booing either. People were curious, and wanted to see what the dashing young king looked like after all these years away.

Diamante could see that the city was stressed. The last twenty years had battered its economy: five years of his high taxes and neglect, almost fifteen years of exploitation by Jalous and the Regnians, seven months of being cut off from exporting their products through La Spezia, and now two weeks of siege. Diamante remembered Varano as a glorious, vibrant, and prosperous place. For two decades, the leaders of the country had taken for granted that it always would be. He was glad that he had not waged a traditional siege–at least there was no starvation or disease.

The street opened into a square, and was as crowded with people as any place Diamante had ever seen. They must have begun arriving the night before to stake out their spots. They were packed shoulder-to-shoulder on the ground, and in every tree, window, and rooftop.

His escort turned into the doorway of a building just at the edge of the square and led him up two flights of stairs to a room with a large balcony. In it were the representatives of Regno and Jalous. They looked tense and hostile. Diamante wondered whether Jakob had been right about this plan.

An arrogant Regnian official stepped forward. He stared at Diamante with obvious contempt. "I don't believe that you are royal. To my eye you don't even appear to be noble. I don't know who you really are, but I promise you this: if you incite a riot, you will be the first to die. As agreed, you have thirty minutes. Afterward you will be escorted to the gate and your traitorous rabble will withdraw from this valley by sundown. Otherwise, I swear by the gods that the Crown of Regno will see you hang and the crows pick at your flesh."

Diamante nodded his head.

There was no ceremony or introduction. The Regnian official gestured impatiently toward the balcony and hissed at Diamante as he walked toward it. "Thirty minutes."

CHAPTER 36

He looked two floors above him to the crowd on the roofs and two floors below to the crowd on the pavement. Though he was no great orator, he spoke as loudly as he could. Thousands strained to hear his words.

"I am a child of Monte Saggezza. Its water and soil run in my veins, as they do in yours. I was born to her freedoms, nurtured by her prosperity, educated in her customs, and entrusted with her future. Just as you were.

"But I was given more, and more was expected of me. When I was a child, I thought that was unjust. Who had a right to expect more of me? The politicians? The people? I resented those expectations. I rebelled against them. I rejected the standards which my father, the people, and our traditions placed upon me. I would be my own man, beholden to none.

"Fifteen years ago, I left Monte Saggezza. I did not choose to leave, although in a way I already had. But I was carried to a distant land, and while there, I learned something important.

"We are our best when we serve with gratitude, not shackled to tradition, or pressed by duty, or to meet the expectations of others. No, we are most noble, most worthy, when we give to others—in love because our hearts are overflowing with what has been given to us by our family, by our community, by the kindness of strangers, by the generations who have sacrificed before us, and by God. When we reflect upon all this good bestowed upon us, it is right to want to share it with others, to serve as we have been served, to give as we have been given to, and to love as we have been loved. I once waited for gratitude to appear inside me, like a feeling. Today, I realize that it is a choice to be made, every day. This is what I learned in that distant country."

Diamante then told them, briefly, the story of his exile, his rebirth in the mines, his learning of new trades as he traveled back, and his life as an apprentice gardener under Master Verde since returning. He told them how he had found the best of what Monte Saggezza was in the busyness and trade of La Spezia, in the piety and industry of the Abbey, in the discipline and generosity of the Verde family, and in the hard work and cheerful spirits of the laborers he worked with everyday. He told them how he had married a woman who had worked to create a small business empire, and who fiercely loved her adopted country. He told them about discovering a son he never knew he had, and how concerned he was for the generation that was growing up never knowing what Monte Saggezza had been–and could still be.

"I betrayed my family's legacy and I betrayed you. You rejected me, and rightfully so. But you did not reject our past, and you did not mean to toss aside our future. You deserved better, and tried to find it. This, however, is not it. If each of us will serve each other with gratitude and grace, we can be a better nation.

"I am King Bonum's son. I have the Sword of Ferox, although I agreed to enter your city today unarmed. I will display it outside the gates for any of you who doubt me. By law and tradition, I am the rightful king of Monte Saggezza. But I do not ask you to support me because of a lineage. We must be done with the claims of privilege and power."

At that moment, an arrow was released from one of the balconies from the north. It pierced Diamante in the right shoulder, just outside the bone–not a life-threatening wound. He fell to his knees, clinging to his shoulder. One man rushed to his aid and covered the bleeding. At the same time, those in the balcony of the archer seized the would-be assassin and threw him to his death.

Diamante rose to his feet.

"Enough!" Enough death for our nation!

"I ask you to free yourselves. Choose liberty and the rule of law. If, by God's favor and your will, I should ever serve again as king, I promise you that I will only do so under a new constitution for Monte Saggezza. It will bind us in a covenant that will dictate the rights and responsibilities of all Saggezzans. It will limit the power of kings in order to prevent them from becoming tyrants. Government will be of the people, but the people will be protected from the government. Each citizen will be free to live their life and pursue happiness and prosperity as they see fit. If you will free yourselves, we will together enumerate and defend the values which God, our forefathers, our land, and our heritage have given us.

"And now I have another reason to be grateful, for you have been gracious enough to hear me. We are involved in a war, but it is a dispute among brothers and sisters. I will withdraw my troops from your valley and leave you to decide what is best for your families and your city.

"Thank you."

He finished, with no flourish or wave. He turned and walked back inside. The crowd did not applaud, nor shout him down. It was subdued. By the clock inside, Diamante estimated that he had spoken for no more than twenty minutes.

The surly Regnian official thrust his face upwards at Diamante's like an angry dog. "We've met your demand and you've had your moment. Now get out of this valley by sundown."

The soldiers again formed an escort around him as he exited the building and marched him quickly back out the way he had come in. The crowds stared intensely at him. A few cheered and a few shouted insults, but mostly they seemed perplexed. There were no farewells at the gate. The entourage stopped, the gate opened, Diamante walked out and it slammed shut behind him.

"See, I told you they couldn't be trusted. Another six inches and this would be different story," Jakob barked as he dressed Diamante's wound.

"What good is my sacrifice if it costs me nothing?" said Diamante.

That afternoon, Diamante's army withdrew from around Varano as promised. They set up a new camp between the hills, near a town that had given its support to his cause. Diamante, however, set up his headquarters on the ridge between the two valleys.

"Now what?" grumbled Jakob as they looked at Varano in the distance below.

"I don't know," Diamante shrugged. "We wait for events to unfold, and then take whatever opportunities God gives us."

"This is not how Feroxans fight a war."

Diamante laughed and slapped him on the shoulder. "This is not Ferox."

They camped on the ridge for three nights. It rained most of the time, and the officers were bored and restless. They asked Diamante how long they would wait here. The army was encamped in the valley behind them, wet, cold, and irritated. The troops were volunteer militia, and absent some assignment or action, wanted to go home. Diamante replied that they would wait until something happened.

On the fourth day, it did. They saw activity around the walls. The gates were open, and soldiers and wagons were organizing outside, as if preparing for a march. Jakob and the officers began barking orders to messengers, alerting their own troops to prepare for an attack. Diamante was quiet and kept watching. Something didn't seem right. It wasn't enough force to be any sort of attack. In fact, it appeared to be no more than half the number of troops he and his staff had estimated to be garrisoned in the city. There were also large numbers of civilians gathering with them, along with wagons and carriages. Some had what appeared from a distance to be furniture strapped to the top. After about half an hour of preparations in front of the gate, the little column began to march up the road that led out of the valley. The people were bearing the royal standards of King Jalous and the Empire of Regno, but civilians in the column outnumbered soldiers by four to one.

One of Diamante's officers shouted and pointed, and the rest of the headquarters staff passed around the spyglass to confirm what he had seen. None of them could believe it, but there it was: flying from the top of Varano's citadel and gates was, unmistakably, the flag of old King Bonum's royal line.

The people of Varano had made their choice. There were no bloody reprisals, but anyone who wanted to remain loyal to Jalous and Regno was shown the gate and given the opportunity to leave freely. Later that afternoon, a delegation from Varano climbed the ridge to Diamante's headquarters. They brought a letter saying that they wished to live as free Saggezzans, and would support his claim to the throne if he kept his promise to restore their rights and traditions, and create a new constitution that bound the nation together in a common covenant.

CHAPTER 37

The city of Varano wrote a new constitution. It listed the rights, institutions, and traditions upon which the city would be based and which every official would swear an oath to protect. A new council and mayor were elected and each pledged Varano's support to Diamante as long as he served those values and obeyed those laws. They sent messengers throughout Monte Saggezza, informing every city, town, and village of their decision. They also notified the Church and the various abbeys and convents.

Varano was perhaps the most influential city in the nation. Its decision was like a shock-wave that swept through the provinces that—until this point—had resisted the rebellion. Not everyone agreed or followed their lead, but most did. They sent envoys to Diamante to negotiate their support in return for various promises and concessions.

To Jakob's and Aquila's dismay, Diamante didn't accept the pledges outright. He told every delegation that he would not accept their loyalty until he had the opportunity to visit them and meet with the leaders and the people. He wished to listen to their hopes and concerns, and for them to hear him pledge to serve them as king. Within a few weeks he found himself traveling around the country, meeting with politicians, craftsmen, churchmen, farmers, and students. Everywhere he went he listened to their frustrations and needs. He apologized for the ways he had failed them in the past, told them his story, and committed to create a constitution that bound Monte Saggezza together in a covenant based on their traditional rights and responsibilities.

Diamante held nothing back. He was open about his mistakes, the life he had lived since then, and about his plans for the future. They questioned and challenged everything, wondering if this older, more mature Diamante had simply learned to become a salesman and politician. They suspected that he was only telling them what they wanted to hear. He responded with humility and grace.

As Diamante went throughout the cities and towns, older Saggezzans realized what he was doing. He was, finally, fulfilling the ancient responsibility of his royal line to tour the countryside and listen to the people. Neglecting this had cost him the throne, but now he was earning it back.

Aquila accompanied him on these tours, and the people loved and trusted her as well. She told her story of entering Monte Saggezza as a refugee from the conflict in Ferox and having spent fifteen years as a business owner and community leader in La Spezia. She did not share her lineage as daughter of the former king of Ferox. She did not wish to lie, but until she could determine the situation north of the mountains, she was hesitant to create the possibility of conflict between the nations. She had ceased to be Nordvindia the day when Jakob led her to La Spezia, and for the time being she would be known only as Aquila. It was the older Saggezzans who again remembered that the other special responsibility of the Saggezzan kings was to maintain the relationship with Ferox. They wondered what it meant that Diamante now had a Feroxan wife, soon to be a Feroxan queen.

All these years later, he was finally growing into the true king of Monte Saggezza.

By mid-summer, the outcome of the war was obvious to everyone. After Varano had declared its freedom and thrown its support to Diamante, it had ceased to be a war and became more like a popular uprising. The only violence in the country was when towns forcibly expelled the royalists and Regnians in their midst. On the sea, it was a different matter. The Regnian navy tried several times to recapture the Saggezzan ports, and the fighting there was fierce. The new Saggezzan navy had some desperate battles defending their coast and protecting merchant ships that ran the Regnian blockade. But Regno's fortunes were changing; it had ruled so many countries with such a heavy hand that other parts of its empire were in chaos as well. Regno had more valuable lands to defend than Monte Saggezza, and was too distracted to commit significant forces to it.

Diamante and the forces of the free Saggezzan provinces were gathered at the bottom of the valley in which Avigliana sat. They held the main road into the city, just over ten miles away. What remained of the forces and citizens loyal to Jalous and Regno were in and around the city. Aquila, Jakob, and Ragnar were all there, prepared to lead battalions if it came to a fight. Diamante also wondered if there would be a final battle. He had sent a letter requesting a negotiation with Jalous to bring this disastrous conflict to an end. Now they waited for a response.

When it came, it surprised everyone but Diamante. Jalous' letter was not addressed to him; in fact it refused to even mention his name or acknowledge his existence. It was addressed to the representatives of the most prominent cities that had declared their independence. He invited them—and them only—to a conference to negotiate "reforms" in the government.

Diamante's closest friends and most ardent supporters were offended, but he was not. "This isn't really about me," he said with a shrug. "Monte Saggezza must restore itself. It has to stand up for its freedom, traditions, and ideals. If they allow me to serve them, so be it. But the nation has to claim those things for itself. They aren't mine to give or take."

The conference took place in the halls of parliament in Avigliana. The city that once had been so bright and vibrant was now crowded and morose. There were no street vendors or performers, only troops and disarray on every corner. The bright and sometimes funny banners that hung along the streets were faded and torn. The city was tired.

Jalous entered with pomp and protocol. He opened with an address to the delegates in which he proclaimed that he had heard their cries for reform. He blamed the country's problems on the previous regime. The line of King Bonum and Diamante had bankrupted the country's treasury and crippled its institutions. He had labored tirelessly to fix the broken country he had inherited. He had tried to clean up the waste and corruption. The most bizarre moment came when he held a common house broom over his head. He waved it about, which he clearly meant to be dramatic and inspiring but which struck everyone in the hall as strange, as he screeched in his creaky voice.

"My fellow Saggezzans, if we work together we can sweep away the problems that the house of King Bonum left us! Who will sweep with me? Sweep with me!"

The hall was silent for several moments. Then someone—no one was ever sure who—began to giggle. Then somewhere else in the hall someone else also began to chuckle. After a few seconds, the dam broke and the hall burst into open laughter. This was not how Jalous had imagined the moment. He made an angry gesture toward his soldiers, ordering them to go into the hall and do something, anything to stop this disrespect. They hesitated for a moment, looking at the hundreds of representatives from almost every city, town, and village in the country. Then they stood at ease and did nothing.

The laughter quickly shifted to boos. Jalous wobbled and blinked, humiliated. He hiked up his robes, turned, and shuffled out the door behind the stage. The room turned angry, delegates pounding the tables, demanding he return. After a while, several of his cabinet members came out to negotiate terms of surrender.

CHAPTER 38

Diamante and Aquila went to Avigliana, but they did not go up to Castello di San Michele. They rented a guesthouse on one of the small lakes that surrounded the town and had Mario and Tessa brought from the Abbey to join them. It was early June, and it would be a busy summer.

The most urgent matter was a new constitution. Diamante refused to climb the hill to the castle until one was in place. Delegates from every part of the country came to Avigliana to take part in writing it. They spent a month of long days in the halls of parliament debating about Monte Saggezza's values and traditions, trying to craft a document that honored and preserved them. On the twenty-second of July they signed it. The new constitution defined the rights and responsibilities of all Saggezzans. The king was to serve the nation, not the other way around. Parliament's role was specific and limited. Whatever powers were not assigned to the national government were assumed to belong to the people, in their villages, towns, and cities. The constitution made it clear that the Saggezzans were a free people, with the right to be left alone by their government to pursue happiness and prosperity as they wished.

The next day, Diamante was installed as king. Since he was to be a servant of the people, the ceremony began by him receiving the insignia of office in the House of Parliament. A parade of delegates, officials, and ordinary citizens then followed him up the steep road to Castello di San Michele. He pointed out to Mario the very spots where he had escaped arrest and snuck into the caverns. The procession entered the chapel and Diamante, having sworn an oath before the people to serve the nation, swore an oath before God to be a man of integrity. After a banquet in the castle's great hall, he showed his family the royal apartments where he had grown up and where Admiral Constante had died defending the Sword of Ferox. He and Tessa shared a tear over their warm but painful memories.

It was late July, and after a heavy winter, the passes were finally open. It was time to correct Diamante's failure on that fateful week, at the end of a short summer, when he had nearly frozen to death in a cave.

Three days after the coronation, Diamante strapped the massive Sword of Ferox to his back and walked up the trail through the foothills. As the ancient custom required, he was the only Saggezzan making this trip, but he was not alone. Aquila walked beside him. She was carrying the heirloom that her forefathers had received from Diamante's father, the Counting Box of Monte Saggezza.

Aquila knew that the Feroxan clans gathered near a certain lake every year in late July for games and horse races. As she and Diamante descended into Ferox, they were anxious about how they would be received. Aquila had heard that the country was in chaos. Without safe passage south to the ports and markets for its resources, Ferox had suffered. The king who had murdered her father and gotten Jalous drunk to avoid producing the Counting Box had himself been overthrown. No single chieftain had been able to consolidate the Feroxan tribes, and they had spent the last ten years fighting among themselves and with other northern tribes. Without their protection of the mountain passes, Monte Saggezza had suffered raids on its northern borders from wild tribes and bandits. The foothills below had become a dangerous no man's land, and many farms and villages had been abandoned.

They were intercepted by scouts a full day's walk from the clan gathering. Diamante announced that he was the king of Monte Saggezza, coming to call upon the leader of the Feroxans, and he showed them the sword. Aquila said nothing as they eyed her with suspicion. The scouts sent word ahead and escorted them to the camp.

Since there was no longer any single lord who commanded all the clans, they were brought to a meeting of the chieftains. The guards suspected Aquila was meant to be an interpreter for the Saggezzan king, but when he spoke their language she was asked to stay outside. Diamante whispered to her that it would be all right, and that he had to make his presentation alone. She nodded and sat outside on a stool with her hood over her face, speaking to no one.

Inside, Diamante declared himself the rightful king of Monte Saggezza, and produced the Sword of Ferox to prove it. He told them about what had happened in Monte Saggezza and why no Saggezzan king had visited in fifteen summers. They were quiet as he shared his story and promised them friendship and faithfulness from that point forward.

The warlords looked at each other nervously. Feroxans spent their long, winter evenings in their feasting halls talking about the history of their people. They knew that when the Saggezzan king visited and displayed the

Sword of Ferox, their own king was supposed to display the heirloom gift of the Saggezzans. But they had no king, and their heirloom had been lost for many years.

Diamante asked which one of them was the rightful ruler of Ferox. They shifted uneasily as Diamante looked around the room, but none would meet his eye. One of the clan chiefs asked the Saggezzan king to allow them to confer alone and the others agreed.

Diamante turned as if to leave, but asked if they would first allow him the privilege to introduce his wife, the queen of Monte Saggezza. They looked at each other in surprise, but none of them wanted to be discourteous. They were glad to have a reason to change the subject, and begged him to please bring her in.

Aquila entered. The chiefs smiled pleasantly, but as she removed her hood they were confused. The queen of Monte Saggezza was Feroxan? Who was this woman?

"My lords, I present my wife, the queen of Monte Saggezza. Her name, in our language, is Aquila, a shortened form of our word *aquilonia*."

Now a few brows were furrowed, as they tried to sort out this puzzle.

"When she was born and raised here, her name in your tongue was Nordvindia. Sixteen years ago, she came to our country and built a successful life for herself. She brought with her a family heirloom." Aquila, or Nordvindia, brought out of her cloak the Counting Box of Saggezza.

Eyes opened wide, and the chieftains began shouting at each other. It was a dangerous moment. Diamante and Aquila were alone in a room of armed warlords, in an enemy camp a week's journey from home. One of the chieftains broke the tension by joking about it. "So you two came alone, huh?" Another added, "This would be an easy war to win."

They all broke out in laughter, but Diamante and Aquila stood, with their faces like flint.

A grizzled-looking warrior asked menacingly, "What is to stop us from destroying that little box for good?"

Finally, what appeared to be the eldest chieftain spoke, "What do you two want? Have you come to meddle in Feroxan affairs? Is this an attempt to place this long-exiled daughter on the throne?" Everyone was silent.

Diamante replied, "I have simply come to renew a trust that I had broken many years ago. I speak on behalf of Monte Saggezza and want to renew its kinship with their northern cousins. Both would benefit from this relationship. As for Nordvindia..."

She held her hand up so to speak for herself. "I have come here as the queen of Monte Saggezza and a relative of yours. I have come to encourage you to think of our people no longer as merely neighbors or even distant relatives. To join in a new bond of kinship that would no longer require annual visits and ancient heirlooms. Whoever the clans chose to lead them, and however that is done, is your affair."

Nordvindia opened the box and showed them that the original colored marbles had been replaced by a set of exquisitely cut diamonds. She explained how Diamante had brought these gems back from exile, and that they served to remind him that peace and prosperity were earned and guarded through character, integrity, and hard work.

Sliding the lid back on, Nordvindia laid the box on the floor before the chieftains and told them that it would belong to whomever they elected. But choose they must, for Monte Saggezza could only negotiate with a united Ferox.

Diamante and Aquila left the council and were escorted to a tent that had been provided for them. A feast had been prepared that night in honor of the Saggezzan king's visit. They attended, but it was a strained affair as the chieftains were clearly distracted and whispered among themselves throughout the evening.

The next day, Diamante and Aquila were treated to seats of honor at the games. There was wrestling, horse racing, and combat with wooden weapons. It moved her deeply to see the old Feroxan customs again. Neither of them failed to notice that the clan chiefs were absent from the games all day.

That night, after the public banquet in which the victors were awarded prizes, Diamante and Aquila were summoned to a meeting of the chieftains. The council was arranged in a semi-circle and the Saggezzan monarchs were given seats facing it.

After many formalities, the clan leaders announced a historic decision. Since no clan or chief could stake a legitimate claim to the crown, none of them would. After a thousand years, it was time to change their form of government. Nordvindia would keep the box in trust to see if her marriage with Diamante produced an heir. If it did, then that child would unite the two royal houses under a single crown and hold both the Sword of Ferox and the Counting Box of Saggezza.

CHAPTER 39

After they crossed back over the mountains, Diamante worked tirelessly to set Monte Saggezza on a new course. He kept in mind the legacy of his father, King Bonum, while forging a better Monte Saggezza based on the new constitution.

Many Saggezzans wanted to see Jalous put on trial for his coup and other crimes against the nation. Diamante saw little value in that. Many people had cooperated with his coup and regime over the years, in varying degrees. Jalous was a broken, old man and it would have been right for him and his supporters to face justice. But Diamante thought that trials in every city and town would turn neighbors against neighbors, when everyone needed to be working together to build a new Monte Saggezza. He and the parliament passed a law that gave amnesty to any member of the former regime that would swear an oath to protect and defend the new constitution. Any who would not were given ninety days to leave the country freely or face trial. Most took the oath, and a few left. Jalous appealed to the King of Regno for sanctuary, and he and most of the Regnian nobles boarded a ship in La Spezia, never to return.

Diamante asked Father Thomas to be the pastor of the chapel in Castello di San Michele, but the Abbot politely declined. He felt that he was serving God best in the Abbey. Diamante traveled there frequently to seek his advice and prayers. He had other reasons to visit, as well. He and Tessa concluded that Mario was thriving in the Abbey school, and it was best for him to continue his education there. Tessa's pottery business was becoming successful and she chose to stay living in the artist's colony on the Abbey's land.

Diamante's responsibilities were legion, but he made one of them a personal priority. He immediately began to restore the palace gardens, paying for the work himself out of the fortune in diamonds he had brought back from exile. In fact, because of his story and his personal fortune, people had begun to call him the Diamond King. Now he built a new estate for Master Verde, his sons, and their family on the grounds, and they supervised the reconstruction. King Diamante himself took as much time away from his duties as he could, donning work clothes and tackling projects with the rest of the workers. They were some of the happiest hours in his life.

He also changed the name. They would no longer be the Royal Gardens, or the Palace Gardens, they would be the National Gardens, a public park open to all citizens. He and Aquila placed a large part of their personal fortunes into a trust to maintain them.

Ever since Diamante had been a guest in her inn, Aquila had watched his curious habit of fiddling with a counting box in the evening, as if silently calculating some problem. She had asked him about it many times, but he had always smiled enigmatically, shaken his head, and told her it was a just a meaningless habit he had picked up in exile.

Shortly after they had been married, during the revolution, she pressed him for an answer and would not let him change the subject. She told him that as his wife and queen, she longed to know what was in his heart. Why would he not share this part of himself with her? What secret was he keeping?

Eventually, Diamante told her the reason for his evening ritual. After he left the mines, he had looked through one of the abandoned buildings outside searching for food. He found a Saggezzan counting box which the guards must have used to calculate what the mines produced each day. It had reminded him of home, and he took it to comfort him in his hunger and bewilderment. That night, as he sat by a fire and considered where he might go and what he might do, he used the box to assess his life. He estimated the time that he had spent on things that were worthwhile, about which he had no regrets. Did he seek wisdom? Could he restore his father's legacy? He then estimated how much of his life he had squandered on worthless illusions that lead to depression that had no value to anyone. That night, sitting by a fire not far from the mine, the figure was so lopsided that he fell asleep weeping, as he realized that until that point, his life had been wasted.

He made a vow before God that from that point on he would take an inventory before he slept each night, reflecting on how he had used the hours of his day. He determined that someday he would be able to say that he had reversed the equation; that he had used the majority of his life well.

That first summer, a few days after they had returned from their visit to Ferox, Diamante sat on the terrace outside the royal apartment. It was a warm evening near the end of July, and between the stars above and the lights of Avigliana below there was nothing but darkness. Braziers lit the terrace, and Diamante remembered that night when his father had told him about the Seven Noble Tenants. It was late, and he was tired and ready for bed. He reached into his bag and pulled out his old counting box, the very one he had found outside the mine. He sipped some hot, spiced wine and reflected on the day, deftly moving the marbles as he figured whether he had used his time well or not.

Aquila stood in the doorway, watching him. She turned and went back inside. A few moments later she walked quietly out onto the terrace and put her hand on his shoulder. He looked up to see her holding the heirloom, the royal Saggezzan Counting Box which they had just brought back from Ferox. As she had told the clan chiefs, Diamante had replaced the marbles inside with beautifully cut diamonds. She offered it to him.

"Use this one, my love." Diamante smiled, but shook his head. "No, that box doesn't belong to me. If it is anyone's, it is yours." She leaned down, kissed him, and whispered in his ear, "Not anymore. I can think of no better use for one of the two heirlooms of the united Houses of Saggezza and Ferox." She took his hand and rested it on her abdomen. His eyes went wide. "Do you mean...?"

"Yes. The Diamond King will have an heir."

CHAPTER 40

It was 5 a.m.

The house was cold and Dad's voice was hoarse. We'd brewed two pots of coffee through the course of the night. I was wired and my butt was numb.

"And...? Then what?" I asked as I stood to stretch.

"I don't know," Dad replied as he walked to the kitchen and poured the dregs into his mug. "My dad would never tell me. Whenever I asked—and I did a lot when I was a kid, before I was sick of the story—he'd say I wasn't ready to learn the rest. I hadn't learned the lessons of the Diamond King."

"What did that mean?" I was rummaging through the cupboard, hoping he had a box of stale donuts or something.

"Your grandfather always dangled this mystery in front of me. That if I learned the lessons of the story, someday I would learn the rest of the story. That I'd inherit the legacy, find my life's purpose, attain my destiny. Stuff like that. It was exciting when I was eight. But by the time I was eighteen I'd had enough. I decided that he was a nut, like the people who devote their life to searching for Atlantis, or the Loch Ness Monster."

I thought about everything that was crammed into my daypack. The documents, receipts, thank you cards. Not to mention the box. It made me think there was something more to all this than a hoax.

"So...what were the lessons of the story? Were you supposed to figure them out for yourself? Or did he tell you?"

"Oh, he told me. Over and over. He made me go through and explain how different elements within the story illustrated the lessons."

"What were they?"

Dad was leaning against the sink, drinking the last of the coffee. Through the window behind him, the sky to the east was turning a lighter shade of black. "There were several, and they all had names. The Heart of Wisdom, The Way of Wealth, The Seven Temptations of Youth, The Seven Noble Tenants of Saggezza."

He shrugged, and began to recite them from memory.

"The Heart of Wisdom is a verse from the ancient scriptures. 'Teach us to number our days aright, that we may gain a heart of wisdom.' In the story, that's what Diamante learned in the mine, and why he used the counting box every night to account for his time. If we understand how precious our days and hours are we will invest them in things that matter. The hours we spend seeking wisdom will lead to a legacy. Our hours spent living an illusion will lead to depression, a place devoid of gratitude. I was so sick of hearing my father say those words." My dad paused for a moment and then he spoke again.

"The Way of Wealth is also from the scriptures. It goes, 'The wealthiest man in the world is the one who has made himself nothing, the man who has poured himself out to serve others, the man who does nothing out of selfish ambition or vain conceit.' Obviously, that's what Diamante had to learn in the story, and why he called himself the wealthiest man in the world."

I thought about the hundreds of thousands—who knows, maybe millions—of dollars' worth of diamonds in my daypack, lying on the kitchen table between us. And the documents that suggested that Grandpa had scattered a fortune in scholarships, grants, and direct aid around the world during his lifetime.

Dad closed his eyes, recalling the next lesson. "The Seven Temptations of Youth are the things that led Diamante astray, before he went into exile. 'They are illusions,' my dad used to say. When I became a teenager and began to resent of him, he would shake his finger at me and tell me that they were more than illusions, they were lies. Lies that leave us broken and disappointed in life if we believe them.

"The Seven Temptations of Youth are Talent, Temperament, Theatrics, Treachery, Trendiness, Toxicity, and Tunnel Vision. Talent is over-rated and misleading. It doesn't guarantee success, and even if the talented person becomes successful, he or she is subject to failure if talent exceeds character. Diamante was talented, but so immature that his talent led him astray because he relied on ability rather than wisdom.

"Temperamental young people obsess about and are led by their feelings. Following feelings without wisdom leads to foolish mistakes and drives other people away. After his exile, Diamante learned to be steady-tempered, and to choose his feelings, not to let his feelings choose his actions.

"Theatrical behavior is especially tempting to the young. Immaturity longs for a stage, for fame. Diamante loved to pose and perform to get attention. After his exile, he cared more about character and accomplishment than glory.

"Treacherous people can be any age, but treachery is a sign of instability. When we don't value people, or our word, or God's grace to us, we will betray others for the sensation of benefitting ourselves. Diamante had no concept of loyalty until he gave up his selfish, vain ambitions.

"Trendy is what young people aspire to be. They value being fashionable and contemporary. Diamante loved being part of the crowd so much that he ignored and destroyed his country's traditions.

"Toxic substances are exciting. They are forbidden fruit, and we are drawn to them as a way to rebel and show our independence. Toxic relationships, behaviors, and situations are a dangerous temptation for young people. Diamante loved the thrill of being bad, of causing trouble for himself or others. He came to learn that real happiness is found in giving blessings to others, not heartaches."

And finally, "To have tunnel vision is to limit your view to your own perspective. But success depends on seeing through other people's eyes. Before his exile, Diamante was unable to see the forest for the trees. He never understood how one decision for himself impacted the entire nation."

Dad fell quiet. I was thinking about how many of those delusions had ruled my life, and what I had to show for them. I wondered if my dad was thinking the same thing, or just stewing in his resentment that his father had beat him over the head with them for eighteen years.

The sky over the neighbor's garage was now charcoal gray. Dad sighed heavily and drained the last of his coffee.

"Anyway, the last lesson was The Seven Noble Tenants of Saggezza. They're sort of the opposite of The Seven Temptations of Youth: Thankful, Thoughtful, Teachable, Truthful, Tenacious, Transparent and Trustworthy. You probably can see how they apply to the story.

"Thankful means that gratitude is the beginning of wisdom. Diamante learned to appreciate his life in the depths of the mine as he sat there broken and appreciative for all that he once had. 'Gratitude is the foundation of life,' my father would say. I guess, because I never started there, he never thought I would learn the rest.

"Thoughtful means that we should take the time to think through our decisions. Our decisions to care about others, consider the community's well-being ahead of our own. Diamante learned to measure his actions by their impact on other people and that those decisions take time to think through. That's why he would invest his time by thinking through and accounting for his hours each day.

"Teachable means that we are not only willing to learn, but that we are capable of learning. That we will submit ourselves to the leadership and discipline of a mentor, as Diamante did under Master Verde. 'The wise man can learn from the fool, but the fool cannot learn from the wise man,' my father would say.

"Truthful is not only the right thing to be; it's the smart thing to be. The truth floats. It always rises to the top. What's done in the dark will always come out in the light. As hard as Diamante tried to hide his mistakes, they always found him.

"Tenacious people never give up. Giving up was not an option. Even though it could have benefitted his level of comfort, or even alleviated his pain, Diamante never quit. Quitting is not an option.

"Transparency is a way of opening ourselves to a greater degree of growth, without hidden agendas and secret sections of our life that eventually conflict with each other. It was only when Diamante was transparent with his mentor, his pastor, and those he loved that he began to grow into the king he would become.

"Trustworthy means just what it says, that we are worthy of being trusted. Diamante didn't deserve to be trusted; he had to earn it. In the end, he did what he said he would do and a kingdom trusted him for it. Trust requires risk on everyone's part. It should never be taken for granted."

The sky had lightened enough that I could see the yard outside. Dawn was not far away. A robin swooped down and stuck his beak into the ground to receive the promise that his early arrival had earned.

"Well, now you know what I know. But you've only had to hear the story and the lessons once. I had to listen to them hundreds of times." Dad was quiet for a moment. "If I'm honest, I have to say that I spent most of my life running away from them. I came to believe that the Diamond King and Saggezza are just legends, but my dad believed in them with every fiber of his being. His job took him on business trips around the world, and the Diamond King fantasy gave it a sense of purpose, I suppose. In my opinion, it was a false purpose, like spending your life looking for the Holy Grail, but it gave him meaning. I turned my back on it all, but I didn't replace it with anything. I never took up the Saggezzan legacy that he kept promising I was destined for. As I think about it, I actually envy him. He lived for something, crazy as it may have been. I haven't."

Dad opened the refrigerator and stared inside. "I'm hungry. Want some eggs?"

CHAPTER 41

A few minutes later, we were eating scrambled eggs and bacon, with another pot of coffee. "So," Dad said between bites, "did you find what you were looking for? Did any part of what I told you help you to make sense out of what Grandpa sent you?"

I finished scraping my plate and leaned back in my chair. I looked my dad in the eye for a long time. I thought about the life he had lived, keeping his distance from his father and everyone else, and for the first time I think I began to understand him. Grandpa had raised him to believe that he had a special destiny, that he was being prepared to inherit a secret legacy and a historic mission. Somewhere in his teenage angst and rebellion he had stopped believing it. I didn't know how or why, and I suspect that he didn't either, but for some reason he came to the conclusion that he had been lied to. And, like a priest who stops believing in God, or a soldier who stops believing in his country, my dad became angry and resentful. He determined that he would never let himself be fooled again. And so he had never believed in anything, or anyone, ever again. He never let himself get close enough or invest his heart too much.

I watched the sunlight clear the top of his neighbor's garage, and it suddenly became clear to me. Deep down inside, probably so deep that he didn't admit it to himself, my dad wanted the story of the Diamond King to be true. That's why it hurt him so much to believe that it wasn't.

I pulled my backpack toward me from the other side of the table. I opened the top, reached past the files, down to the bottom, and pulled the box. I gently laid it on the table in front of us. Dad looked puzzled as he saw the plain wooden box in front of him. He picked it up, his hands trembling; he slowly turned it over to examine the bottom, just to see if there might be a crest, a mark, a sign, something. It was there. He took a deep breath. I kept my eyes on him as he opened the lid. I could see the reflection of the twelve enormous diamonds in his eyes. I could see shock, followed by confusion, followed by recognition. Then I saw tears.

In my whole life I had never imagined my father crying. Silent tears became great heaving sobs. He cried like a child, moaning from the depths of his soul. The dam broke, and a lifetime of hurt washed over both of us. I found myself crying with him. For him missing out on his father's legacy, for their broken relationship, for having never known Grandpa myself, for Mom's hurt and our broken family, for the struggles in my own life and business, and my fear of bankruptcy. For all that should have and could have been in our lives.

We examined the box together. It was hard to believe that this was actually the box from the story, one of the two heirlooms of the united Crown of Saggezza and Ferox. That conclusion raised more questions than it answered. I spread out the documents I had brought, and we went through them carefully, trying to make sense of the paper trail.

Dad said that Grandpa never seemed to have an extraordinary amount of money. They lived a comfortable, upper-middle class lifestyle in keeping with Grandpa's job as a consultant for an international engineering firm that took him on two or three business trips a month. He had no idea where the money had come from, for all of the philanthropy and charity work Grandpa obviously did. We took out a calculator and it added up to over eighty million dollars, spread among scholarships, clean-water projects in poor villages, micro-business investments for women in developing countries, and a dozen other things. And, I had only grabbed the files for the last ten years.

Clearly, the Saggezza Foundation was the clue, whatever that was. Dad walked over to his computer. I looked over his shoulder as we searched for anything that I might have missed. All we found were the same contradictory rumors on dubious websites. Like the flying saucers at Area 51 or the treasure of the Freemasons, there were only guesses but no evidence.

The only viable lead that we found was from Grandpa's letter to me. We read through it together:

Dear Grandson,

If you are receiving this letter, then I have passed on and my grateful life has come to an end. Today I pass on to you all that I know. Take the knowledge that I once possessed and enjoy the life I once had. Become the wealthiest man in the world.

When you're ready, take the heirloom to Sacra di San Michele.

If you father is still alive, please let him know that I never stopped loving him.

— Your Affectionate Grandfather.

P.S. Forever remember the legacy of the Diamond King

We googled "Sacra di San Michele" and found that it was a real place in northern Italy, not far from the Alps. Could this be the place from the story? Wikipedia said that Sacra di San Michele had been a monastery and is now a church, and that it was open to tourists for visits. Wiki also said that the location has been in use from at least Roman times, and probably much earlier. Structures had been built and rebuilt many times over the ages, for any number of purposes. Clearly, the heirloom Grandpa mentioned in the letter must be the box. I guessed that it meant that when I was ready, I was supposed to take the box to this place in Italy and...do what?

But was I ready? How could I tell?

My dad had an answer. "I think that your grandfather would want you to think about the story and the lessons. Examine yourself according to the lessons. Have you learned The Heart of Wisdom, The Way of Wealth? Are you aware of The Seven Temptations of Youth, and can you apply The Seven Noble Tenants of Saggezza?"

"Of course not."

Dad leaned forward, and for the first time I could remember since I was maybe ten years old, he put his arm around my shoulders. "Grandpa meant for me to learn the story and apply the lessons. I see now that he hoped that I would learn them well enough so that he could pass all of this on to me. I didn't."

"Son, listen carefully. You have learned them. Not by hearing them and trying to master them, like Grandpa wanted me to. I wasn't capable of becoming that person. You already are that man. You embody everything that Grandpa tried teaching me better than anyone I've ever known."

He went back to the computer and reopened his web browser. He started typing and clicking through menus while I thought about what he'd said.

"What are you doing?"

"I'm booking you a flight to Italy. You need to go to Sacra di San Michele."

"Dad, I'm embarrassed to say this, but I can't afford a trip like that right now. My credit card doesn't have enough room on it to fill my truck with gas."

He waved me off. "Don't worry about it. This is on me. This has been my life's mystery. I have to know how it turns out."

"Umm, OK," I replied, wondering how I would explain this to Amanda and my employees.

"Tell your wife that you have to go out of town to take care of his estate. Tell her I gave you the money."

I thought for a moment. That was true. I just might get away with that. But I had another thought.

"Dad, I'm just going to tell her the truth." He looked at me and smiled. "Of course."

"And Dad, book it for both of us. You have to come with me."

He looked regretful. "Your grandfather didn't invite me."

"Well, I am. If he's trusted me enough to leave all of this to me, then I must be trustworthy enough to make some of these decisions for myself. What am I supposed to do when I get there? There might be clues I'm supposed to solve. I don't know the story like you do. I need you along to help me figure them out."

CHAPTER 42

I had never been out of the country before and didn't even have a passport. My dad gave me the money to rush order one. I told Amanda what my dad suggested, that my dad and I had gone through Grandpa's boxes and papers in the garage, and found that we had to go to Italy to take care of some issues related to his estate.

"Did he leave you any money?" She smiled that smile that always makes my problems seem unimportant. "A big pile of money? An estate in Italy?" She was joking, mostly. She was hoping that maybe I had inherited enough to rescue us and our business from bankruptcy. I told her that I wasn't sure, but that Dad and I were going to find out what this was all about.

"If anyone can do it, you can." Her support was unwavering.

A week later we arrived in Avigliana, Italy. We pulled off the highway, following the GPS in the tiny European rental car past a pretty, little lake. Cottages and bed and breakfast places dotted the shore. Overhead, on a steep hill which was more like a crag, was a massive stone structure. It looked like a castle to me, but the guidebook insisted it was a monastery and church.

The road zigzagged up the hill, past beautiful homes overlooking the valley. We saw an endless stream of bicycle racers riding slowly up or speeding down. There was a parking area at the top, next to a little restaurant. A man and his son sold fresh produce from a cart. There were tourist signs in French, Spanish, Italian, and English. The signs posted the admission price to tour the facility, and asked tourists to please respect the schedule; that this was still a functioning church.

We walked up a little footpath and emerged at the base of the monastery. We went through the gate in the massive stone walls that seemed to rise right up out of the earth and climbed a steep, stone stairway. I was out of breath by the time we got to the top. We emerged on a sort of terrace, with more walls and towers rising above us in layers, like a massive wedding cake. I used to joke with friends that I wasn't afraid of heights, but that it was the falling to my death part that freaked me out. This wasn't the most comfortable spot I'd ever been in. The Alps towered over us, and more than a thousand feet below us the red roofs of the town came up to the edge of the lake we had passed earlier. The terrace seemed to hang there in space.

There were signs directing us to a small building on the first level. Reading the English version of the signs, apparently attendance for mass was free, but tours of the facility required a ticket to help maintain the place. We followed the other tourists into the ticket office and gift shop. Inside, a college-aged girl sat behind a desk selling tickets and handing out maps. While we waited in line, I looked at the souvenirs and wondered what we were supposed to do now that we were here.

The tourists ahead of us left, and we were alone with the girl behind the counter. Dad gave her some euros, and folding open a map, she pointed out the tour route and where the restrooms were located. Thankfully, she spoke English.

I was totally out of my element. I tried to sound chatty and casual as I told her that we were visiting from America. She smiled politely, but I realized that I had just told her something she had probably figured out on her own. Sticking with my chit-chat strategy, I said that we had read about this place on the Internet. Polite as ever, she nodded, but I could tell she was probably thinking about what she was going to do after she got off work.

"Yeah," I said, "it seemed like an interesting place, and we were passing through the area, so we thought we'd check it out." The pretty, young Italian girl kept on nodding, bored out of her mind. "So many interesting stories and legends. It said that Julius Caesar came through here, and Hannibal with the elephants."

At the other end of the gift shop, a middle-aged man came in carrying a fresh batch of the tour maps. *He must work here,* I thought. He was dressed casually, but in that sharp way that I was realizing Europeans make look so easy. He was scrolling through some high-tech looking cell phone, reading his text messages perhaps. He started thumb-typing a reply while he waited for us to leave.

The girl was blinking her beautiful eyelashes, probably pleading in morse code with the other employee to rescue her from this dorky American.

"You know, I read on the Web that this place has something to do with the Saggezza Foundation." I paused, nodded my head. Nothing. "You ever hear anything about that?" The girl had pretty eyes, but now she was rolling them. In her accented English she replied, "People see it on the Internet. They come here and ask. It is not true. Just Internet stories."

I decided to double down. What did I have to lose? I reached into my daypack and pulled out a piece of paper. I had photocopied and enlarged the crest from one of Grandpa's documents, the same crest that was on the bottom of the box. I asked her if she had ever seen anything like this before, and if it had anything to do with the monastery.

She shook her head. She clearly had no idea what it was. I thanked her and took my ticket. I guess we'd have to wander around and look for clues. Maybe there was a secret doorway somewhere, or a code in the artwork. I was improvising.

As I started to turn, I ran into the middle-aged man. He had been standing behind me, and had seen over my shoulder the paper I had put onto the counter. He looked concerned.

"*Scusi, Signore.* I am the manager here. May I ask, where did you get that paper? Was that from the Internet, as well?"

I figured I might as well be truthful. That was one of the Seven Noble Tenants, wasn't it? "No, as a matter of fact, I got it from my grandfather. He just passed away, and these are from some papers he left me."

He looked at me strangely for a while. Then he said deliberately, "I am sorry to hear of your loss. Were you close to your grandfather?"

"Actually, I wasn't."

"Ah," said the manager, "that is sad. I do not know how your grandfather got that piece of paper, but there are many false documents on the Internet, we see many of these hoaxes."

"I don't think my grandfather got that crest off the Internet."

"Perhaps he got it from someone else who did, *signore*."

I didn't know what else to do, so I decided to go all in. "Well, see that's the thing. That's only a photocopy I made. He had hundreds of documents with that crest, embossed on old paper. And on...certain objects that he left to me as well."

"What sort of objects, *signore?*" The manager was probably a heck of a poker player. I couldn't see any reaction at all. Maybe he knew something, or maybe he thought I was a nut and was humoring me. You couldn't tell by looking at him.

"Well, this, for one." I pulled the box out of my pack, but didn't open it. I just showed him the same crest that had been on the paper.

There was just a little twitch at the corner of his right eye. There it was. His "tell." He knew something. And he knew that I knew that he knew something.

He set the maps down on the corner of the counter, and I think he asked the girl with pretty eyes to stock them into the racks, because that's what she started doing.

"Would you be so kind as to follow me?"

I stuffed the box back into my pack and my dad and I shrugged at each other. We followed him out.

CHAPTER 43

We followed the manager downstairs to an office area full of worn cubicles and file cabinets. There were maybe half a dozen people working there. From what I could tell, this was the operations office for the place. There were brochures and posters, some tour guide uniforms hanging on the wall, and a couple of guides standing around, waiting for tours to start. We walked past a desk, where someone was working at a computer, ordering cleaning supplies.

We went into an office toward the back where the manager seated us in front of his desk and asked if we would like some coffee. He left and in a few minutes came back with some espresso cups and little biscotti cookies on saucers. He closed the door.

"My name is Mr. Tomaselli. I am the, how should I say it, the director, of Sacra di San Michele. Please, tell me about yourself, and your grandfather."

I introduced myself and my father. Briefly, I told him about how my father had become estranged from his father, and Mr. Tomaselli looked genuinely sad and nodded to my dad, who acknowledged him with a nod back. I told him about myself, my family, and my business and how it had been difficult lately with the economy. I told him about coming home and finding the packages on my porch, about discovering the contents and going to my dad to ask for help in figuring it out. I told him about hearing the story of the Diamond King and the lessons.

Mr. Tomaselli paid careful attention, but said nothing until I finished. He thought for a moment. "And why have you come here?"

I reached in my pack and pulled out the letter from Grandpa, and handed it to him. He read it slowly.

"It says, 'When you're ready, take the heirloom to Sacra di San Michele.' I don't think that I'm ready, but my father does. He convinced me to come here. If I'm understanding all of this correctly, I'm supposed to bring this here." I pulled out the box and opened the lid, showing him the diamonds. "I have no idea what's supposed to happen now."

Mr. Tomaselli rose slowly, and then bowed his head. "*Scusi.*"

He went to the side wall in his office and lifted an oil painting off the wall. Behind, just like in the movies, was a safe. He spun the combination and opened it. He was standing in front, so I couldn't see inside, but he reached in and lifted something very large out. As he turned, I could see that it was a leather case. He set it on the desk and undid the clasps.

"*Signore,* I believe that this belongs to you. For now."

He handed me a fierce-looking broadsword, made of some dull, gray metal.

My dad and I were stunned. The story was true? How could that be? Why didn't all of this appear in history books? If it was real, how was it all obscured in a legend?

Mr. Tomaselli reached under his desk and pushed a button; the bookcase swung aside, revealing a door in the stone wall behind it.

"*Signori,* would you come with me, please?"

I grabbed the sword and my dad picked up the box. We walked through the door and found another set of offices, very different from the ones we had just been through. It was a gleaming, high-tech place, with a couple dozen people working, mostly on computers or talking on wireless headsets. Big flat-screen monitors on the walls were following the global financial markets.

They all stopped and stared as Dad and I walked through, carrying the Royal Counting Box and the Sword of Ferox. Mr. Tomaselli paused, and waved at the room. "*Signori,* may I introduce you to the Saggezza Foundation."

We went into a glass-walled conference room and were served more coffee and biscotti. On the table was a guest book. Mr. Tomaselli flipped over a couple pages and I examined the names. I came to the last signature. It was my grandfather's. Above it was my great-grandfather and so on. Mr. Tomaselli motioned for my dad to come over and handed him a very ornate pen. Sir? Clearly he wanted my dad to sign the register. He did with no questions asked. Mr. Tomaselli extended his hand to me and my dad handed me the pen. Now my hands were shaking. A million thoughts raced through my mind. Was I able, could I handle it? With a deep breath and the words of my wife "If anyone can..." I signed my name.

Mr. Tomaselli's senior staff members came in and were introduced. I was stunned, and I sat there with the box and the sword on the conference room table in front of me next to the book. Mr. Tomaselli stood at the front and began a briefing, illustrating his points by using a remote to control the video screens on the walls. Dad and I finally got all our questions answered.

Diamante and Aquila (or Nordvindia) had an heir who united the crowns of Monte Saggezza and Ferox. Their fortunes were shrewdly invested in a trust, and their son and then their granddaughter had multiplied those investments. The charter was very specific. Every year the majority of the earnings from the ever-growing Saggezza fortune was to be used to equip and empower bright young people to make the world a better place. The rest was reinvested so that the trust fund would grow and, over time, have even more resources for philanthropy and charity. Mr. Tomaselli talked about just some of the hundreds of types of projects around the world that the money had gone to over the centuries. I was astonished. There were wonderful things that had taken place throughout history because of a grant or seed money from the Saggezza fortune. In fact, many of the world's most famous non-profit organizations were started with anonymous donations from the Saggezza Foundation.

A few generations after Diamante and Aquila, world events had rendered Monte Saggezza, Ferox, and their form of government obsolete. Empires rose and fell around them, and wars, disasters, migrations, and politics buried them in a forgotten past. But the fortune lived on. Their granddaughter had foreseen these changes and had set up the Saggezza Foundation. Each generation, the director passed their mantle on, along with the story, the lessons, and all the wisdom and experience that the directors had accumulated over the centuries. The Box and the Sword were their signs of office.

"But, I don't understand," I interrupted. "I thought that you, Mr. Tomaselli, are the director."

"No, *signore*. I am the director of Sacra di San Michele, and I manage the Foundation's operations. We manage the Foundation's fortune, provide security, and so forth. We also, of course, dispense the funds according to the director's instructions. Your grandfather was the director of the Saggezza Foundation. Now you are."

"Why me? Why was I chosen?"

"You received the envelope with your name on it from within one of the boxes. The envelope with the articles and items." Mr. Tomaselli raised his eyebrows in question.

"Yes–but that hardly answers the question."

"Your Grandfather believed that your life resembled the Seven Saggezza tenants.

"Please help me," I responded in a little tired frustration.

"My pleasure. Your grandfather and I have had many discussions as to why and when you would be ready. I believe he has made the right choice.

"The first item is the article you wrote for your high school newspaper. You have always taken the time to think about others. Taking time to think is the first and most important tenant of all the character traits. Thinking through and making wise decisions is key to carrying out the others. Without thinking about your life and taking into account your hours and the time you spend, the other traits will rarely develop. 'Think About It' was an article that always impressed your grandfather.

"The second items were the thank-you cards. A trait your father required of you, that you seem to have taken on as a faithful trait. Your grandfather cherished the thank you cards you gave him.

"Third, a report card from your professor who happened to be a good friend of your grandfather. The fact that you ask good questions reveals that you are teachable. Good grades are one thing but to be teachable is a character trait that is far more necessary after you graduate.

"Next, a silver dollar. You probably were too young to know what your grandfather was doing but he left that silver dollar next to the couch to test your honesty. You have a tendency of telling the truth. Your grandfather noticed it at an early age.

"You're probably wondering how we obtained the Internet report and a copy of the loan you paid off."

I agreed that I was a little more than curious.

"We own both the Internet company and the bank where you do business. The Internet report reveals the opportunity for transparency. Meeting with your friends on Friday morning will be strengthened when you begin to share more openly. You have nothing to be ashamed of. The bank note reveals your integrity. You did what you said you would do. It is that simple.

"And the article about the baseball game..."

I interrupted, "Tenacity, right?"

Mr. Tomaselli smiled.

"Correct. We have yet to see you give up. I hope we never do. Use these pictures and items to remember the seven tenants."

"Ok." I took a deep breath and tried to take it all in. I walked over to the nearest chair and sat down. Nobody said anything. We all knew it was a lot to handle all at once.

I looked back at Mr. Tomaselli.

My dad walked over and put his hand on my shoulder. "You OK?"

I smiled and shrugged my shoulders and looked back at Mr. Tomaselli.

"Now what? What do I do?"

"Your role is to lead, and to empower the leaders around you." Mr. Tomaselli explained that the rules of the Foundation required that the fortune be used for charitable investments, not to enrich the director. Obviously, if the Foundation's existence or the size of its fortune were known, the Foundation would be subject to pressure and politics and would be unable to fulfill its mission of being an anonymous charity. For that reason, the director was sworn to secrecy and given a job that made it possible for him or her to travel the world without attracting attention.

Therefore, said Mr. Tomaselli, I would be given a position as a consultant—much like my grandfather—in one of the many corporations that the Foundation owned stock in. It would not be too demanding and would leave me ample time to do my work, seeking out worthy projects to give money to. My grandfather had been set up as a consultant for a global engineering company. Perhaps, Mr. Tomaselli asked, I would prefer something in computers? Or construction?

"You mean a cover identity, like what the CIA does?"

Mr. Tomaselli and his staffed actually laughed. "The CIA is..." he paused. "They've been doing this for fifty years. We've been doing it for centuries."

He grew serious again. "Please understand: the Saggezza Foundation does not allow us to become personally wealthy. It is to be used for serving others. Your job will provide for your family and allow you to perform your duties without financial anxiety, but you will not become rich through this work.

"Let me get this straight. The Saggezza Foundation gives me a job where I don't have to work too hard, have unlimited travel resources, and I spend my life going around finding worthwhile people and projects to give money away to? I just let you know which ones and you get the money to them?"

Mr. Tomaselli appeared deeply concerned, almost angry. "Your grandfather did not leave you the lottery. He left you a legacy. The people you empower will be given the opportunity to shape their communities. Maybe even make history. They will dramatically impact the lives around them.

"There are a couple more rules you must understand. You much give at least twenty percent of the funds to twelve different organizations each year. I do believe that you might find it a bit more challenging that you think."

"How much money are we talking?"

Mr. Tomaselli nodded to one of his staff, who clicked something on a laptop, bringing up some figures on one of the screens. "At the moment, with current real-time market valuations, the Foundation's total assets stand at $4.7 billion US dollars."

I had to move past that. I simply couldn't process it.

"One final rule. You may not be away from your family more than ten days a month.

My dad stood up, nearly shouting, "My father was gone all the time! He was never home. When did the rules change?"

Mr. Tomaselli didn't flinch. "The rules have never changed. Your father, my close friend, was never gone more than ten days a month. Sometimes our memories are the illusions we believed as children to defend the childish decisions we make as adults."

My dad sat back down as if to concede defeat.

Mr. Tomaselli walked over to his desk and pulled out a small envelope and walked over to my father. "This is for you."

My dad opened the envelope and read quietly. Tears once again rolled down his cheeks as he buried his face in his hands.

I walked over and put my hand on his back. After a while he gathered himself and looked up and smiled. "He knew I'd show up. He never stopped believing in me"

I thought for a moment.

"Mr. Tomaselli, as the director, how much freedom do I have in how I go about my work?"

"You have freedom within the rules, of course. The Box goes with you, for you to use daily. The sword stays here, for safekeeping. You may share the secret with your immediate family, at your discretion, as we do not condone lying to your loved ones. There is a budget of what you can give away, based on fund earnings of the previous year." He shrugged. "Beyond that, you have much discretion."

I made my first decision as director. "My father shall assist me in my work. The previous director, my grandfather, had always dreamed of giving this role to his son. It has passed to me, and I accept it. But to honor my grandfather and to help me accomplish more, my father will assist me." In a less confident voice I asked, "Is there any reason why I can't do that?"

I felt my father's hand grab my knee under the table, and he cleared his throat. I knew him well enough to tell that he was suppressing a sob.

Mr. Tomaselli and his staff talked for a few moments in Italian. Some nodded and some shook their heads, but in the end most of them shrugged. Mr. Tomaselli turned toward us. "No reason that we can think of. We shall make sure that he has sufficient resources to accomplish his work."

"So where do we start?" I asked Mr. Tomaselli. He thought for a moment.

"There is a small non-profit organization finding mentors for kids in Grand Rapids, Michigan. I think they could use our help. Check it out; it will be a good place for you to start."

I could go on and tell you of all the wonderful people I have met, the lives that have been changed, and the unsung leaders that have been empowering the powerless for years. But for now....

That is how I became the wealthiest man in the world.

Roy A. Clark

Special Thanks to:

Rich DeVos who taught me at a conference...

Leaders lead; if they can't lead they attempt to manage everything. Once they realize they can no longer manage, they make excuses. But once they run out of excuses they blame, and once they blame, they rarely lead again.

Joe Tomaselli for his amazing grace.

All my teachers, leaders, dreamers, mentors, pastors and friends, I just can't say it enough...thank you for all you have done and continue to do for me.

Dirk Roskam on whose laptop I write. You have achieved your goal of giving and I am wealthier for it.

Thank you all.

Made in the USA
Charleston, SC
27 February 2011